Anonymous

Out of Mulberry Street

Stories of Tenement Life in New York City

Anonymous

Out of Mulberry Street
Stories of Tenement Life in New York City

ISBN/EAN: 9783337414795

Printed in Europe, USA, Canada, Australia, Japan

Cover: Foto ©Andreas Hilbeck / pixelio.de

More available books at **www.hansebooks.com**

Out of Mulberry Street

Stories of tenement
life in New York City

By

Jacob A. Riis

Author of " How the Other Half Lives,"
"'The Children of the Poor," etc.

New York
The Century Co.
1898

PREFACE

SINCE I wrote "How the Other Half Lives" I have been asked many times upon what basis of experience, of fact, I built that account of life in New York tenements. These stories contain the answer. They are from the daily grist of the police hopper in Mulberry street, at which I have been grinding for twenty years. They are reprinted from the columns of my newspaper, and from the magazines as a contribution to the discussion of the lives and homes of the poor, which in recent years has done much to better their lot, and is yet to do much more when we have all come to understand each other. In this discussion only facts are of value, and these stories are true. In the few instances in which I have taken the ordering of events into my own hands, it is chiefly their sequence with which I have interfered. The facts themselves remain as I found them.

J. A. R.

301 MULBERRY STREET.

CONTENTS

CONTENTS

OUT OF
MULBERRY STREET

MERRY CHRISTMAS IN THE TENEMENTS

I T was just a sprig of holly, with scarlet berries showing against the green, stuck in, by one of the office boys probably, behind the sign that pointed the way up to the editorial rooms. There was no reason why it should have made me start when I came suddenly upon it at the turn of the stairs; but it did. Perhaps it was because that dingy hall, given over to dust and drafts all the days of the year, was the last place in which I expected to meet with any sign of Christmas; perhaps it was because I myself had nearly forgotten the holiday. Whatever the cause, it gave me quite a turn.

I stood, and stared at it. It looked dry, almost withered. Probably it had come a long way. Not much holly grows about

1   1

Printing-House Square, except in the colored supplements, and that is scarcely of a
kind to stir tender memories. Withered and
dry, this did. I thought, with a twinge of
conscience, of secret little conclaves of my
children, of private views of things hidden
from mama at the bottom of drawers, of
wild flights when papa appeared unbidden in
the door, which I had allowed for once to
pass unheeded. Absorbed in the business of
the office, I had hardly thought of Christmas
coming on, until now it was here. And this
sprig of holly on the wall that had come to
remind me,—come nobody knew how far,—
did it grow yet in the beech-wood clearings,
as it did when I gathered it as a boy, track-
ing through the snow? "Christ-thorn" we
called it in our Danish tongue. The red berries, to our simple faith, were the drops of
blood that fell from the Saviour's brow as it
drooped under its cruel crown upon the cross.

Back to the long ago wandered my
thoughts: to the moss-grown beech in which
I cut my name and that of a little girl with
yellow curls, of blessed memory, with the first
jack-knife I ever owned; to the story-book
with the little fir-tree that pined because it
was small, and because the hare jumped over

it, and would not be content though the wind
and the sun kissed it, and the dews wept over
it and told it to rejoice in its young life; and
that was so proud when, in the second year,
the hare had to go round it, because then it
knew it was getting big,—Hans Christian
Andersen's story that we loved above all the
rest; for we knew the tree right well, and the
hare; even the tracks it left in the snow we
had seen. Ah, those were the Yule-tide sea-
sons, when the old Domkirke shone with a
thousand wax candles on Christmas eve; when
all business was laid aside to let the world
make merry one whole week; when big red
apples were roasted on the stove, and bigger
doughnuts were baked within it for the long
feast! Never such had been known since.
Christmas to-day is but a name, a memory.

A door slammed below, and let in the noises
of the street. The holly rustled in the draft.
Some one going out said, "A Merry Christmas to you all!" in a big, hearty voice. I
awoke from my reverie to find myself back in
New York with a glad glow at the heart. It
was not true. I had only forgotten. It was
myself that had changed, not Christmas.
That was here, with the old cheer, the old
message of good-will, the old royal road to

the heart of mankind. How often had I seen its blessed charity, that never corrupts, make light in the hovels of darkness and despair! how often watched its spirit of self sacrifice and devotion in those who had, besides themselves, nothing to give! and as often the sight had made whole my faith in human nature. No! Christmas was not of the past, its spirit not dead. The lad who fixed the sprig of holly on the stairs knew it; my reporter's note-book bore witness to it. Witness of my contrition for the wrong I did the gentle spirit of the holiday, here let the book tell the story of one Christmas in the tenements of the poor:

It is evening in Grand street. The shops east and west are pouring forth their swarms of workers. Street and sidewalk are filled with an eager throng of young men and women, chatting gaily, and elbowing the jam of holiday shoppers that linger about the big stores. The street-cars labor along, loaded down to the steps with passengers carrying bundles of every size and odd shape. Along the curb a string of peddlers hawk penny toys in push-carts with noisy clamor, fearless for once of being moved on by the police.

Christmas brings a two weeks' respite from
persecution even to the friendless street-fakir.
From the window of one brilliantly lighted
store a bevy of mature dolls in dishabille
stretch forth their arms appealingly to a
troop of factory-hands passing by. The
young men chaff the girls, who shriek with
laughter and run. The policeman on the corner stops beating his hands together to keep
warm, and makes a mock attempt to catch
them, whereat their shrieks rise shriller than
ever. "Them stockin's o' yourn 'll be the
death o' Santa Claus!" he shouts after them,
as they dodge. And they, looking back, snap
saucily, "Mind yer business, freshy!" But
their laughter belies their words. "They
gin it to ye straight that time," grins the
grocer's clerk, come out to snatch a look at
the crowds; and the two swap holiday greet-
ings.

At the corner, where two opposing tides of
travel form an eddy, the line of push-carts de-
bouches down the darker side-street. In its
gloom their torches burn with a fitful glare
that wakes black shadows among the trusses
of the railroad structure overhead. A woman,
with worn shawl drawn tightly about head
and shoulders, bargains with a peddler for a

monkey on a stick and two cents' worth of flitter-gold. Five ill-clad youngsters flatten their noses against the frozen pane of the toy-shop, in ecstasy at something there, which proves to be a milk-wagon, with driver, horses, and cans that can be unloaded. It is something their minds can grasp. One comes forth with a penny goldfish of pasteboard clutched tightly in his hand, and, casting cautious glances right and left, speeds across the way to the door of a tenement, where a little girl stands waiting. "It's yer Chris'mas, Kate," he says, and thrusts it into her eager fist. The black doorway swallows them up.

Across the narrow yard, in the basement of the rear house, the lights of a Christmas tree show against the grimy window-pane. The hare would never have gone around it, it is so very small. The two children are busily engaged fixing the goldfish upon one of its branches. Three little candles that burn there shed light upon a scene of utmost desolation. The room is black with smoke and dirt. In the middle of the floor oozes an oil-stove that serves at once to take the raw edge off the cold and to cook the meals by. Half the window-panes are broken, and the holes stuffed

with rags. The sleeve of an old coat hangs
out of one, and beats drearily upon the sash
when the wind sweeps over the fence and
rattles the rotten shutters. The family wash,
clammy and gray, hangs on a clothes-line
stretched across the room. Under it, at a
table set with cracked and empty plates, a
discouraged woman sits eying the children's
show gloomily. It is evident that she has
been drinking. The peaked faces of the little
ones wear a famished look. There are three
—the third an infant, put to bed in what was
once a baby-carriage. The two from the street
are pulling it around to get the tree in range.
The baby sees it, and crows with delight. The
boy shakes a branch, and the goldfish leaps
and sparkles in the candle-light.

"See, sister!" he pipes; "see Santa Claus!"
And they clap their hands in glee. The woman
at the table wakes out of her stupor, gazes
around her, and bursts into a fit of maudlin
weeping.

The door falls to. Five flights up, another
opens upon a bare attic room which a patient
little woman is setting to rights. There are
only three chairs, a box, and a bedstead in the
room, but they take a deal of careful arrang-
ing. The bed hides the broken plaster in the

wall through which the wind came in; each chair-leg stands over a rat-hole, at once to hide it and to keep the rats out. One is left; the box is for that. The plaster of the ceiling is held up with pasteboard patches. I know the story of that attic. It is one of cruel desertion. The woman's husband is even now living in plenty with the creature for whom he forsook her, not a dozen blocks away, while she "keeps the home together for the childer." She sought justice, but the lawyer demanded a retainer; so she gave it up, and went back to her little ones. For this room that barely keeps the winter wind out she pays four dollars a month, and is behind with the rent. There is scarce bread in the house; but the spirit of Christmas has found her attic. Against a broken wall is tacked a hemlock branch, the leavings of the corner grocer's fitting-block; pink string from the packing-counter hangs on it in festoons. A tallow dip on the box furnishes the illumination. The children sit up in bed, and watch it with shining eyes.

"We 're having Christmas!" they say.

The lights of the Bowery glow like a myriad twinkling stars upon the ceaseless flood of humanity that surges ever through the great highway of the homeless. They shine upon long rows of lodging-houses, in which hundreds of young men, cast helpless upon the reef of the strange city, are learning their first lessons of utter loneliness; for what desolation is there like that of the careless crowd when all the world rejoices? They shine upon the tempter, setting his snares there, and upon the missionary and the Salvation Army lass, disputing his catch with him; upon the police detective going his rounds with coldly observant eye intent upon the outcome of the contest; upon the wreck that is past hope, and upon the youth pausing on the verge of the pit in which the other has long ceased to struggle. Sights and sounds of Christmas there are in plenty in the Bowery. Juniper and tamarack and fir stand in groves along the busy thoroughfare, and garlands of green embower mission and dive impartially. Once a year the old street recalls its youth with an effort. It is true that it is largely a commercial effort—that the evergreen, with an instinct that is not of its native hills, haunts saloon-corners by preference; but the smell of the pine-woods is in the air, and—Christmas is not too critical—one is grateful for the effort. It varies with the opportunity.

At "Beefsteak John's" it is content with
artistically embalming crullers and mince-pies
in green cabbage under the window lamp.
Over yonder, where the mile-post of the old
lane still stands,—in its unhonored old age
become the vehicle of publishing the latest
"sure cure" to the world,—a florist, whose
undenominational zeal for the holiday and
trade outstrips alike distinction of creed and
property, has transformed the sidewalk and
the ugly railroad structure into a veritable
bower, spanning it with a canopy of green,
under which dwell with him, in neighborly
good-will, the Young Men's Christian Associ-
ation and the Gentile tailor next door.

In the next block a "turkey-shoot" is in
progress. Crowds are trying their luck at
breaking the glass balls that dance upon tiny
jets of water in front of a marine view with
the moon rising, yellow and big, out of a silver
sea. A man-of-war, with lights burning aloft,
labors under a rocky coast. Groggy sailor-
men, on shore leave, make unsteady attempts
upon the dancing balls. One mistakes the
moon for the target, but is discovered in season. "Don't shoot that," says the man who
loads the guns; "there's a lamp behind it."
Three scared birds in the window-recess try

vainly to snatch a moment's sleep between
shots and the trains that go roaring over-head
on the elevated road. Roused by the sharp
crack of the rifles, they blink at the lights in
the street, and peck moodily at a crust in
their bed of shavings.

The dime-museum gong clatters out its
noisy warning that "the lecture" is about to
begin. From the concert-hall, where men sit
drinking beer in clouds of smoke, comes the
thin voice of a short-skirted singer warbling,
"Do they think of me at home?" The young
fellow who sits near the door, abstractedly
making figures in the wet track of the
"schooners," buries something there with a
sudden restless turn, and calls for another
beer. Out in the street a band strikes up.
A host with banners advances, chanting an
unfamiliar hymn. In the ranks marches a
cripple on crutches. Newsboys follow, gap-
ing. Under the illuminated clock of the
Cooper Institute the procession halts, and the
leader, turning his face to the sky, offers a
prayer. The passing crowds stop to listen.
A few bare their heads. The devoted group,
the flapping banners, and the changing torch-
light on upturned faces, make a strange,
weird picture. Then the drum-beat, and the

band files into its barracks across the street.
A few of the listeners follow, among them
the lad from the concert-hall, who slinks
shamefacedly in when he thinks no one is
looking.

Down at the foot of the Bowery is the
"pan-handlers' beat," where the saloons elbow
one another at every step, crowding out all
other business than that of keeping lodgers
to support them. Within call of it, across
the square, stands a church which, in the
memory of men yet living, was built to shelter the fashionable Baptist audiences of a
day when Madison Square was out in the
fields, and Harlem had a foreign sound. The
fashionable audiences are gone long since.
To-day the church, fallen into premature de-
cay, but still handsome in its strong and noble
lines, stands as a missionary outpost in the
land of the enemy, its builders would have
said, doing a greater work than they planned.
To-night is the Christmas festival of its Eng-
lish-speaking Sunday-school, and the pews are
filled. The banners of United Italy, of modern Hellas, of France and Germany and Eng-
land, hang side by side with the Chinese
dragon and the starry flag—signs of the
cosmopolitan character of the congregation.

Greek and Roman Catholics, Jews and joss-
worshipers, go there; few Protestants, and
no Baptists. It is easy to pick out the children in their seats by nationality, and as easy
to read the story of poverty and suffering that
stands written in more than one mother's
haggard face, now beaming with pleasure at
the little ones' glee. A gaily decorated Christmas tree has taken the place of the pulpit.
At its foot is stacked a mountain of bundles,
Santa Claus's gifts to the school. A self-con-
scious young man with soap-locks has just
been allowed to retire, amid tumultuous applause, after blowing "Nearer, my God, to
thee" on his horn until his cheeks swelled
almost to bursting. A trumpet ever takes
the Fourth Ward by storm. A class of little
girls is climbing upon the platform. Each
wears a capital letter on her breast, and has
a piece to speak that begins with the letter;
together they spell its lesson. There is momentary consternation: one is missing. As
the discovery is made, a child pushes past the
doorkeeper, hot and breathless. "I am in
'Boundless Love,'" she says, and makes for
the platform, where her arrival restores con-
fidence and the language.

In the audience the befrocked visitor from

up-town sits cheek by jowl with the pigtailed
Chinaman and the dark-browed Italian.   Up
in ¦the gallery, farthest from the preacher's
desk and the tree, sits a Jewish mother with
three boys, almost in rags.   A dingy and
threadbare shawl partly hides her poor calico
wrap and patched apron.   The woman shrinks
in the pew, fearful of being seen; her boys
stand upon the benches, and applaud with the
rest.   She endeavors vainly to restrain them.
" Tick, tick !" goes the old clock over the door
through which wealth and fashion went out
long years ago, and poverty came in.

Tick, tick! the world moves, with us—
without; without or with.   She is the yesterday, they the to-morrow.   What shall the
harvest be ?

Loudly ticked the old clock in time with
the doxology, the other day, when they
cleared the tenants out of Gotham Court
down here in Cherry street, and shut the iron
doors of Single and Double Alley against
them.   Never did the world move faster or
surer toward a better day than when the
wretched slum was seized by the health-
officers as a nuisance unfit longer to disgrace
a Christian city.   The snow lies deep in the
deserted passageways, and the vacant floors

are given over to evil smells, and to the rats
that forage in squads, burrowing in the neg-
lected sewers. The "wall of wrath" still
towers above the buildings in the adjoining
Alderman's Court, but its wrath at last is
wasted.

It was built by a vengeful Quaker, whom
the alderman had knocked down in a quarrel over the boundary-line, and transmitted
its legacy of hate to generations yet unborn;
for where it stood it shut out sunlight and
air from the tenements of Alderman's Court.
And at last it is to go, Gotham Court and
all; and to the going the wall of wrath has
contributed its share, thus in the end aton-
ing for some of the harm it wrought. Tick!
old clock; the world moves. Never yet did
Christmas seem less dark on Cherry Hill
than since the lights were put out in Gotham
Court forever.

In "the Bend" the philanthropist undertaker who "buries for what he can catch on
the plate" hails the Yule-tide season with a
pyramid of green made of two coffins set on
end. It has been a good day, he says cheer-
fully, putting up the shutters; and his mind
is easy. But the "good days" of the Bend
are over, too. The Bend itself is all but gone.

Where the old pigsty stood, children dance and
sing to the strumming of a cracked piano-
organ propelled on wheels by an Italian and
his wife. The park that has come to take the
place of the slum will curtail the undertaker's
profits, as it has lessened the work of the police. Murder was the fashion of the day that
is past. Scarce a knife has been drawn since
the sunlight shone into that evil spot, and
grass and green shrubs took the place of the
old rookeries. The Christmas gospel of peace
and good-will moves in where the slum moves
out. It never had a chance before.

The children follow the organ, stepping in
the slush to the music,—bareheaded and wit'
torn shoes, but happy,—across the Five Poin
and through "the Bay,"—known to the dire
tory as Baxter street,—to "the Divide," still
Chatham street to its denizens though the
aldermen have rechristened it Park Row.
There other delegations of Greek and Italian
children meet and escort the music on its
homeward trip. In one of the crooked streets
near the river its journey comes to an end.
A battered door opens to let it in. A tallow
dip burns sleepily on the creaking stairs. The
water runs with a loud clatter in the sink: it
is to keep it from freezing. There is not a

whole window-pane in the hall. Time was when this was a fine house harboring wealth and refinement. It has neither now. In the old parlor down-stairs a knot of hard-faced men and women sit on benches about a deal table, playing cards. They have a jug between them, from which they drink by turns. On the stump of a mantel-shelf a lamp burns before a rude print of the Mother of God. No one pays any heed to the hand-organ man and his wife as they climb to their attic. There is a colony of them up there—three families four rooms.

." "Come in, Antonio," says the tenant of the ʾouble flat,—the one with two rooms,—"come d keep Christmas." Antonio enters, cap in ɪnd. In the corner by the dormer-window a "crib" has been fitted up in commemoration of the Nativity. A soap-box and two hemlock branches are the elements. Six tallow candles and a night-light illuminate a singular collection of rarities, set out with much ceremonial show. A doll tightly wrapped in swaddling-clothes represents "the Child." Over it stands a ferocious-looking beast, easily recognized as a survival of the last political campaign,—the Tammany tiger,— threatening to swallow it at a gulp if one as

2

much as takes one's eyes off it. A miniature
Santa Claus, a pasteboard monkey, and several other articles of bric-à-brac of the kind
the tenement affords, complete the outfit. The
background is a picture of St. Donato, their
village saint, with the Madonna "whom they
worship most." But the incongruity harbors
no suggestion of disrespect. The children
view the strange show with genuine reverence,
bowing and crossing themselves before it.
There are five, the oldest a girl of seventeen,
who works for a sweater, making three dollars
a week. It is all the money that comes in, for
the father has been sick and unable to work
eight months and the mother has her hands
full: the youngest is a baby in arms. Three
of the children go to a charity school, where
they are fed, a great help, now the holidays
have come to make work slack for sister. The
rent is six dollars—two weeks' pay out of the
four. The mention of a possible chance of
light work for the man brings the daughter
with her sewing from the adjoining room,
eager to hear. That would be Christmas indeed! "Pietro!" She runs to the neighbors
to communicate the joyful tidings. Pietro
comes, with his new-born baby, which he is
tending while his wife lies ill, to look at the

maestro, so powerful and good. He also has been out of work for months, with a family of mouths to fill, and nothing coming in. His children are all small yet, but they speak English.

"What," I say, holding a silver dime up before the oldest, a smart little chap of seven —"what would you do if I gave you this?"

"Get change," he replies promptly. When he is told that it is his own, to buy toys with, his eyes open wide with wondering incredulity. By degrees he understands. The father does not. He looks questioningly from one to the other. When told, his respect increases visibly for "the rich gentleman."

They were villagers of the same community in southern Italy, these people and others in the tenements thereabouts, and they moved their patron saint with them. They cluster about his worship here, but the worship is more than an empty form. He typifies to them the old neighborliness of home, the spirit of mutual help, of charity, and of the common cause against the common enemy. The community life survives through their saint in the far city to an unsuspected extent. The sick are cared for; the dreaded hospital is fenced out. There are no Italian evictions.

The saint has paid the rent of this attic through two hard months; and here at his shrine the Calabrian village gathers, in the persons of these three, to do him honor on Christmas eve.

Where the old Africa has been made over into a modern Italy, since King Humbert's cohorts struck the up-town trail, three hundred of the little foreigners are having an uproarious time over their Christmas tree in the Children's Aid Society's school. And well they may, for the like has not been seen in Sullivan street in this generation. Christmas trees are rather rarer over here than on the East Side, where the German leavens the lump with his loyalty to home traditions. This is loaded with silver and gold and toys without end, until there is little left of the original green. Santa Claus's sleigh must have been upset in a snow-drift over here, and righted by throwing the cargo overboard, for there is at least a wagon-load of things that can find no room on the tree. The appearance of "teacher" with a double armful of curly-headed dolls in red, yellow, and green Mother-Hubbards, doubtful how to dispose of them, provokes a shout of approval, which is presently quieted by the principal's

bell. School is "in" for the preliminary exercises. Afterward there are to be the tree
and ice-cream for the good children. In their
anxiety to prove their title clear, they sit so
straight, with arms folded, that the whole
row bends over backward. The lesson is
brief, the answers to the point.

"What do we receive at Christmas?" the
teacher wants to know. The whole school
responds with a shout, "Dolls and toys!"
To the question, "Why do we receive them
at Christmas?" the answer is not so prompt.
But one youngster from Thompson street
holds up his hand. He knows. "Because
we always get 'em," he says; and the class is
convinced: it is a fact. A baby wails because
it cannot get the whole tree at once. The
"little mother"—herself a child of less than
a dozen winters—who has it in charge cooes
over it, and soothes its grief with the aid of a
surreptitious sponge-cake evolved from the
depths of teacher's pocket. Babies are en-
couraged in these schools, though not origi-
nally included in their plan, as often the one
condition upon which the older children can
be reached. Some one has to mind the baby,
with all hands out at work.

The school sings "Santa Lucia" and "Children of the Heavenly King," and baby is lulled to sleep.

"Who is this King?" asks the teacher, suddenly, at the end of a verse. Momentary stupefaction. The little minds are on ice-cream just then; the lad nearest the door has telegraphed that it is being carried up in pails. A little fellow on the back seat saves the day. Up goes his brown fist.

"Well, Vito, who is he?"

"McKinley!" shouts the lad, who remembers the election just past; and the school adjourns for ice-cream.

It is a sight to see them eat it. In a score of such schools, from the Hook to Harlem, the sight is enjoyed in Christmas week by the men and women who, out of their own pockets, reimburse Santa Claus for his outlay, and count it a joy—as well they may; for their beneficence sometimes makes the one bright spot in lives that have suffered of all wrongs the most cruel—that of being despoiled of their childhood. Sometimes they are little Bohemians; sometimes the children of refugee Jews; and again, Italians, or the descendants of the Irish stock of Hell's Kitchen and Poverty Row; always the poorest, the shabbiest, the hungriest—the children Santa

Claus loves best to find, if any one will show him the way. Having so much on hand, he has no time, you see, to look them up himself. That must be done for him; and it is done. To the teacher in this Sullivan-street school came one little girl, this last Christmas, with anxious inquiry if it was true that he came around with toys.

"I hanged my stocking last time," she said, "and he did n't come at all." In the front house indeed, he left a drum and a doll, but no message from him reached the rear house in the alley. "Maybe he could n't find it," she said soberly. Did the teacher think he would come if she wrote to him? She had learned to write.

Together they composed a note to Santa Claus, speaking for a doll and a bell—the bell to play "go to school" with when she was kept home minding the baby. Lest he should by any chance miss the alley in spite of directions, little Rosa was invited to hang her stocking, and her sister's, with the janitor's children's in the school. And lo! on Christmas morning there was a gorgeous doll, and a bell that was a whole curriculum in itself, as good as a year's schooling any day! Faith in Santa Claus is established in that Thomp-

son-street alley for this generation at least;
and Santa Claus, got by hook or by crook into
an Eighth-Ward alley, is as good as the whole
Supreme Court bench, with the Court of Appeals thrown in, for backing the Board of
Health against the slum.

But the ice-cream! They eat it off the
seats, half of them kneeling or squatting on
the floor; they blow on it, and put it in their
pockets to carry home to baby. Two little
shavers discovered to be feeding each other,
each watching the smack develop on the
other's lips as the acme of his own bliss, are
"cousins"; that is why. Of cake there is a
double supply. It is a dozen years since
"Fighting Mary," the wildest child in the
Seventh-Avenue school, taught them a lesson
there which they have never forgotten. She
was perfectly untamable, fighting everybody
in school, the despair of her teacher, till on
Thanksgiving, reluctantly included in the general amnesty and mince-pie, she was caught
cramming the pie into her pocket, after eying
it with a look of pure ecstasy, but refusing to
touch it. "For mother" was her explanation, delivered with a defiant look before
which the class quailed. It is recorded, but
not in the minutes, that the board of man-

agers wept over Fighting Mary, who, all un-
conscious of having caused such an astonish-
ing "break," was at that moment engaged in
maintaining her prestige and reputation by
fighting the gang in the next block. The
minutes contain merely a formal resolution to
the effect that occasions of mince-pie shall
carry double rations thenceforth. And the
rule has been kept—not only in Seventh-Avenue, but in every industrial school—since.
Fighting Mary won the biggest fight of her
troubled life that day, without striking a
blow.

It was in the Seventh-Avenue school last
Christmas that I offered the truant class a
four-bladed penknife as a prize for whittling
out the truest Maltese cross. It was a class
of black sheep, and it was the blackest sheep
of the flock that won the prize. "That awful
Savarese," said the principal in despair. I
thought of Fighting Mary, and bade her take
heart. I regret to say that within a week the
hapless Savarese was black-listed for banking
up the school door with snow, so that not even
the janitor could get out and at him.

Within hail of the Sullivan-street school
camps a scattered little band, the Christmas
customs of which I had been trying for years

to surprise. They are Indians, a handful of Mohawks and Iroquois, whom some ill wind has blown down from their Canadian reservation, and left in these West-Side tenements to eke out such a living as they can weaving mats and baskets, and threading glass pearls on slippers and pin-cushions, until, one after another, they have died off and gone to happier hunting-grounds than Thompson street. There were as many families as one could count on the fingers of both hands when I first came upon them, at the death of old Tamenund, the basket-maker. Last Christmas there were seven. I had about made up my mind that the only real Americans in New York did not keep the holiday at all, when, one Christmas eve, they showed me how. Just as dark was setting in, old Mrs. Benoit came from her Hudson-street attic—where she was known among the neighbors, as old and poor as she, as Mrs. Ben Wah, and believed to be the relict of a warrior of the name of Benjamin Wah—to the office of the Charity Organization Society, with a bundle for a friend who had helped her over a rough spot—the rent, I suppose. The bundle was done up elaborately in blue cheese-cloth, and contained a lot of little garments which she

had made out of the remnants of blankets and
cloth of her own from a younger and better
day. "For those," she said, in her French
patois, "who are poorer than myself"; and
hobbled away. I found out, a few days later,
when I took her picture weaving mats in her
attic room, that she had scarcely food in the
house that Christmas day and not the car-fare
to take her to church! Walking was bad,
and her old limbs were stiff. She sat by
the window through the winter evening, and
watched the sun go down behind the western
hills, comforted by her pipe. Mrs. Ben Wah,
to give her her local name, is not really an
Indian; but her husband was one, and she
lived all her life with the tribe till she came
here. She is a philosopher in her own quaint
way. "It is no disgrace to be poor," said she
to me, regarding her empty tobacco-pouch;
"but it is sometimes a great inconvenience."
Not even the recollection of the vote of cen-
sure that was passed upon me once by the
ladies of the Charitable Ten for surrep-
titiously supplying an aged couple, the special
object of their charity, with army plug, could
have deterred me from taking the hint.

Very likely, my old friend Miss Sherman, in
her Broome-street cellar,—it is always the

attic or the cellar,—would object to Mrs. Ben
Wah's claim to being the only real American
in my note-book. She is from down East,
and says "stun" for stone. In her youth she
was lady's-maid to a general's wife, the recollection of which military career equally con-
dones the cellar and prevents her holding any
sort of communication with her common
neighbors, who add to the offense of being
foreigners the unpardonable one of being
mostly men. Eight cats bear her steady company, and keep alive her starved affections.
I found them on last Christmas eve behind
barricaded doors; for the cold that had locked
the water-pipes had brought the neighbors
down to the cellar, where Miss Sherman's
cunning had kept them from freezing. Their
tin pans and buckets were even then bang-
ing against her door. "They 're a miserable
lot," said the old maid, fondling her cats de-
fiantly; "but let 'em. It 's Christmas. Ah!"
she added, as one of the eight stood up in
her lap and rubbed its cheek against hers,
"they 're innocent. It is n't poor little ani-
mals that does the harm. It 's men and women that does it to each other." I don't
know whether it was just philosophy, like
Mrs. Ben Wah's, or a glimpse of her story.
If she had one, she kept it for her cats.

In a hundred places all over the city, when Christmas comes, as many open-air fairs spring suddenly into life. A kind of Gentile Feast of Tabernacles possesses the tenement districts especially. Green-embowered booths stand in rows at the curb, and the voice of the tin trumpet is heard in the land. The common source of all the show is down by the North River, in the district known as "the Farm." Down there Santa Claus establishes headquarters early in December and until past New Year. The broad quay looks then more like a clearing in a pine-forest than a busy section of the metropolis. The steamers discharge their loads of fir-trees at the piers until they stand stacked mountain-high, with foot-hills of holly and ground-ivy trailing off toward the land side. An army-train of wagons is engaged in carting them away from early morning till late at night; but the green forest grows, in spite of it all, until in places it shuts the shipping out of sight altogether. The air is redolent with the smell of balsam and pine. After nightfall, when the lights are burning in the busy market, and the homeward-bound crowds with baskets and heavy burdens of Christmas greens jostle one another with good-natured banter,—nobody is ever cross down here in the holiday season,—it is good to take a stroll through the Farm, if one has a spot in his heart faithful yet to the hills and the woods in spite of the latter-day city. But it is when the moonlight is upon the water and upon the dark phantom forest, when the heavy breathing of some passing steamer is the only sound that breaks the stillness of the night, and the watchman smokes his only pipe on the bulwark, that the Farm has a mood and an atmosphere all its own, full of poetry, which some day a painter's brush will catch and hold.

Into the ugliest tenement street Christmas brings something of picturesqueness as of cheer. Its message was ever to the poor and the heavy-laden, and by them it is understood with an instinctive yearning to do it honor. In the stiff dignity of the brownstone streets up-town there may be scarce a hint of it. In the homes of the poor it blossoms on stoop and fire-escape, looks out of the front window, and makes the unsightly barber-pole to sprout overnight like an Aaron's rod. Poor indeed is the home that has not its sign of peace over the hearth, be it but a single sprig of green. A little color creeps with it even into rabbinical Hester street, and shows in the shop-win-

dows and in the children's faces. The very
feather-dusters in the peddler's stock take on
brighter hues for the occasion, and the big
knives in the cutler's shop gleam with a lively
anticipation of the impending goose "with
fixin's"—a concession, perhaps, to the commercial rather than the religious holiday:
business comes then, if ever. A crowd of
ragamuffins camp out at a window where
Santa Claus and his wife stand in state, em-
bodiment of the domestic ideal that has not
yet gone out of fashion in these tenements,
gazing hungrily at the announcement that "A
silver present will be given to every purchaser
by a real Santa Claus.—M. Levitsky." Across
the way, in a hole in the wall, two cobblers
are pegging away under an oozy lamp that
makes a yellow splurge on the inky blackness
about them, revealing to the passer-by their
bearded faces, but nothing of the environ-
ment save a single sprig of holly suspended
from the lamp. From what forgotten brake
it came with a message of cheer, a thought of
wife and children across the sea waiting their
summons, God knows. The shop is their
house and home. It was once the hall of the
tenement; but to save space, enough has been
walled in to make room for their bench and

bed. The tenants go through the next house. No matter if they are cramped; by and by they will have room. By and by comes the spring, and with it the steamer. Does not the green branch speak of spring and of hope? The policeman on the beat hears their hammers beat a joyous tattoo past midnight, far into Christmas morning. Who shall say its message has not reached even them in their slum?

Where the noisy trains speed over the iron highway past the second-story windows of Allen street, a cellar door yawns darkly in the shadow of one of the pillars that half block the narrow sidewalk. A dull gleam behind the cobweb-shrouded window-pane supplements the sign over the door, in Yiddish and English: "Old Brasses." Four crooked and moldy steps lead to utter darkness, with no friendly voice to guide the hapless customer. Fumbling along the dank wall, he is left to find the door of the shop as best he can. Not a likely place to encounter the fastidious from the Avenue! Yet ladies in furs and silk find this door and the grim old smith within it. Now and then an artist stumbles upon them, and exults exceedingly in his find. Two holiday shoppers are even now haggling with the coppersmith over the price of a pair of curiously wrought brass candle-sticks. The old man has turned from the forge, at which he was working, unmindful of his callers roving among the dusty shelves. Standing there, erect and sturdy, in his shiny leather apron, hammer in hand, with the firelight upon his venerable head, strong arms bared to the elbow, and the square paper cap pushed back from a thoughtful, knotty brow, he stirs strange fancies. One half expects to see him fashioning a gorget or a sword on his anvil. But his is a more peaceful craft. Nothing more warlike is in sight than a row of brass shields, destined for ornament, not for battle. Dark shadows chase one another by the flickering light among copper kettles of ruddy glow, old-fashioned samovars, and massive andirons of tarnished brass. The bargaining goes on. Overhead the nineteenth century speeds by with rattle and roar; in here linger the shadows of the centuries long dead. The boy at the anvil listens open-mouthed, clutching the bellows-rope.

In Liberty Hall a Jewish wedding is in progress. Liberty! Strange how the word echoes through these sweaters' tenements, where starvation is at home half the time. It is as an all-consuming passion with these

3

people, whose spirit a thousand years of
bondage have not availed to daunt. It
breaks out in strikes, when to strike is to
hunger and die. Not until I stood by a
striking cloakmaker whose last cent was
gone, with not a crust in the house to feed
seven hungry mouths, yet who had voted
vehemently in the meeting that day to keep
up the strike to the bitter end,—bitter indeed,
nor far distant,—and heard him at sunset re-
cite the prayer of his fathers: "Blessed art
thou, O Lord our God, King of the world, that
thou hast redeemed us as thou didst redeem
our fathers, hast delivered us from bondage
to liberty, and from servile dependence to re-
demption!"—not until then did I know what
of sacrifice the word might mean, and how ut-
terly we of another day had forgotten. But
for once shop and tenement are left behind.
Whatever other days may have in store, this
is their day of play, when all may rejoice.

The bridegroom, a cloak-presser in a hired
dress-suit, sits alone and ill at ease at one
end of the hall, sipping whisky with a fine
air of indifference, but glancing apprehensively toward the crowd of women in the
opposite corner that surrounds the bride, a
pale little shop-girl with a pleading, winsome

face. From somewhere unexpectedly appears
a big man in an ill-fitting coat and skull cap,
flanked on either side by a fiddler, who scrapes
away and away, accompanying the improvi-
sator in a plaintive minor key as he halts
before the bride and intones his lay. With
many a shrug of stooping shoulders and
queer excited gesture, he drones, in the harsh,
guttural Yiddish of Hester street, his story
of life's joys and sorrows, its struggles and
victories in the land of promise. The women
listen, nodding and swaying their bodies sym-
pathetically. He works himself into a frenzy,
in which the fiddlers vainly try to keep up
with him. He turns and digs the laggard
angrily in the side without losing the meter.
The climax comes. The bride bursts into
hysterical sobs, while the women wipe their
eyes. A plate, heretofore concealed under his
coat, is whisked out. He has conquered;
the inevitable collection is taken up.

The tuneful procession moves upon the
bridegroom. An Essex-street girl in the
crowd, watching them go, says disdainfully:
"None of this humbug when I get married."
It is the straining of young America at the
fetters of tradition. Ten minutes later, when,
between double files of women holding can-

dles, the couple pass to the canopy where the rabbi waits, she has already forgotten; and when the crunching of a glass under the bridegroom's heel announces that they are one, and that until the broken pieces be reunited he is hers and hers alone, she joins with all the company in the exulting shout of "Mozzel tov!" ("Good luck!"). Then the *dupka*, men and women joining in, forgetting all but the moment, hands on hips, stepping in time, forward, backward, and across. And then the feast.

They sit at the long tables by squads and tribes. Those who belong together sit together. There is no attempt at pairing off for conversation or mutual entertainment, at speech-making or toasting. The business in hand is to eat, and it is attended to. The bridegroom, at the head of the table, with his shiny silk hat on, sets the example; and the guests emulate it with zeal, the men smoking big, strong cigars between mouthfuls. "Gosh! ain't it fine?" is the grateful comment of one curly-headed youngster, bravely attacking his third plate of chicken-stew. "Fine as silk," nods his neighbor in knickerbockers. Christmas, for once, means something to them that they can understand.

The crowd of hurrying waiters make room
for one bearing aloft a small turkey adorned
with much tinsel and many paper flowers.
It is for the bride, the one thing not to be
touched until the next day—one day off from
the drudgery of housekeeping; she, too, can
keep Christmas.

A group of bearded, dark-browed men sit
apart, the rabbi among them. They are the
orthodox, who cannot break bread with the
rest, for fear, though the food be kosher,
the plates have been defiled. They brought
their own to the feast, and sit at their own
table, stern and justified. Did they but know
what depravity is harbored in the impish
mind of the girl yonder, who plans to hang
her stocking overnight by the window! There
is no fireplace in the tenement. Queer things
happen over here, in the strife between the
old and the new. The girls of the College
Settlement, last summer, felt compelled to
explain that the holiday in the country which
they offered some of these children was to be
spent in an Episcopal clergyman's house,
where they had prayers every morning.
"Oh," was the indulgent answer, "they know
it is n't true, so it won't hurt them."

The bell of a neighboring church-tower

strikes the vesper hour. A man in working-clothes uncovers his head reverently, and passes on. Through the vista of green bowers formed of the grocer's stock of Christmas trees a passing glimpse of flaring torches in the distant square is caught. They touch with flame the gilt cross towering high above the "White Garden," as the German residents call Tompkins Square. On the sidewalk the holy-eve fair is in its busiest hour. In the pine-board booths stand rows of staring toy dogs alternately with plaster saints. Red apples and candy are hawked from carts. Peddlers offer colored candles with shrill outcry. A huckster feeding his horse by the curb scatters, unseen, a share for the sparrows. The cross flashes white against the dark sky.

In one of the side-streets near the East River has stood for thirty years a little mission church, called Hope Chapel by its founders, in the brave spirit in which they built it. It has had plenty of use for the spirit since. Of the kind of problems that beset its pastor I caught a glimpse the other day, when, as I entered his room, a rough-looking man went out.

"One of my cares," said Mr. Devins, looking after him with contracted brow. "He

has spent two Christmas days of twenty-three
out of jail. He is a burglar, or was. His
daughter has brought him round. She is a
seamstress. For three months, now, she has
been keeping him and the home, working
nights. If I could only get him a job! He
won't stay honest long without it; but who
wants a burglar for a watchman? And how
can I recommend him?"

A few doors from the chapel an alley sets
into the block. We halted at the mouth of it.

"Come in," said Mr. Devins, "and wish
Blind Jennie a Merry Christmas."

We went in, in single file; there was not
room for two. As we climbed the creaking stairs of the rear tenement, a chorus of
children's shrill voices burst into song somewhere above.

"It is her class," said the pastor of Hope
Chapel, as he stopped on the landing. "They
are all kinds. We never could hope to reach
them; Jennie can. They fetch her the papers
given out in the Sunday-school, and read to
her what is printed under the pictures; and
she tells them the story of it. There is nothing Jennie does n't know about the Bible."

The door opened upon a low-ceiled room,
where the evening shades lay deep. The red
glow from the kitchen stove discovered a jam

of children, young girls mostly, perched on the table, the chairs, in one another's laps, or squatting on the floor; in the midst of them, a little old woman with heavily veiled face, and wan, wrinkled hands folded in her lap. The singing ceased as we stepped across the threshold.

"Be welcome," piped a harsh voice with a singular note of cheerfulness in it. "Whose step is that with you, pastor? I don't know it. He is welcome in Jennie's house, whoever he be. Girls, make him to home." The girls moved up to make room.

"Jennie has not seen since she was a child," said the clergyman, gently; "but she knows a friend without it. Some day she shall see the great Friend in his glory, and then she shall be Blind Jennie no more."

The little woman raised the veil from a face shockingly disfigured, and touched the eyeless sockets. "Some day," she repeated, "Jennie shall see. Not long now—not long!" Her pastor patted her hand. The silence of the dark room was broken by Blind Jennie's voice, rising cracked and quavering: "Alas! and did my Saviour bleed?" The shrill chorus burst in:

It was there by faith I received my sight,
And now I am happy all the day.

The light that falls from the windows of the Neighborhood Guild, in Delancey street, makes a white path across the asphalt pavement. Within there is mirth and laughter. The Tenth Ward Social Reform Club is having its Christmas festival. Its members, poor mothers, scrubwomen,—the president is the janitress of a tenement near by,—have brought their little ones, a few their husbands, to share in the fun. One little girl has to be dragged up to the grab-bag. She cries at the sight of Santa Claus. The baby has drawn a woolly horse. He kisses the toy with a look of ecstatic bliss, and toddles away. At the far end of the hall a game of blindman's-buff is starting up. The aged grandmother, who has watched it with growing excitement, bids one of the settlement workers hold her grandchild, that she may join in; and she does join in, with all the pent-up hunger of fifty joyless years. The worker, looking on, smiles; one has been reached. Thus is the battle against the slum waged and won with the child's play.

Tramp! tramp! comes the to-morrow upon the stage. Two hundred and fifty pairs of little feet, keeping step, are marching to dinner in the Newsboys' Lodging-house. Five hundred pairs more are restlessly awaiting their turn up-stairs. In prison, hospital, and alms-house to-night the city is host, and gives of her plenty. Here an unknown friend has spread a generous repast for the waifs who all the rest of the days shift for themselves as best they can. Turkey, coffee, and pie, with "vegetubles" to fill in. As the file of eagle-eyed youngsters passes down the long tables, there are swift movements of grimy hands, and shirt-waists bulge, ragged coats sag at the pockets. Hardly is the file seated when the plaint rises: "I ain't got no pie! It got swiped on me." Seven despoiled ones hold up their hands.

The superintendent laughs—it is Christmas eve. He taps one tentatively on the bulging shirt. "What have you here, my lad?"

"Me pie," responds he, with an innocent look; "I wuz scart it would get stole."

A little fellow who has been eying one of the visitors attentively takes his knife out of his mouth, and points it at him with con-viction.

"I know you," he pipes. "You 're a p'lice commissioner. I seen yer picter in the papers. You 're Teddy Roosevelt!"

The clatter of knives ceases suddenly. Seven pies creep stealthily over the edge of the table, and are replaced on as many plates. The visitors laugh. It was a case of mistaken identity.

Farthest down-town, where the island narrows toward the Battery, and warehouses crowd the few remaining tenements, the somber-hued colony of Syrians is astir with preparation for the holiday. How comes it that in the only settlement of the real Christmas people in New York the corner saloon appropriates to itself all the outward signs of it? Even the floral cross that is nailed over the door of the Orthodox church is long withered and dead: it has been there since Easter, and it is yet twelve days to Christmas by the belated reckoning of the Greek Church. But if the houses show no sign of the holiday, within there is nothing lacking. The whole colony is gone a-visiting. There are enough of the unorthodox to set the fashion, and the rest follow the custom of the country. The men go from house to house, laugh, shake hands, and kiss one another on both cheeks, with the salutation, "Kol am va antom Salimoon." "Every year and you are safe," the Syrian guide renders it into English; and a non-professional interpreter amends it: "May you

grow happier year by year." Arrack made
from grapes and flavored with aniseed, and
candy baked in little white balls like marbles,
are served with the indispensable cigarette;
for long callers, the pipe.

In a top-floor room of one of the darkest of
the dilapidated tenements, the dusty window-
panes of which the last glow in the winter sky
is tinging faintly with red, a dance is in progress. The guests, most of them fresh from
the hillsides of Mount Lebanon, squat about
the room. A reed-pipe and a tambourine fur-
nish the music. One has the center of the
floor. With a beer-jug filled to the brim on
his head, he skips and sways, bending, twisting, kneeling, gesturing, and keeping time,
while the men clap their hands. He lies down
and turns over, but not a drop is spilled. Another succeeds him, stepping proudly, grace-
fully, furling and unfurling a handkerchief
like a banner. As he sits down, and the beer
goes around, one in the corner, who looks like
a shepherd fresh from his pasture, strikes up
a song—a far-off, lonesome, plaintive lay.
"'Far as the hills,'" says the guide; "a song
of the old days and the old people, now sel-
dom heard." All together croon the refrain.
The host delivers himself of an epic about his

love across the seas, with the most agonizing expression, and in a shockingly bad voice. He is the worst singer I ever heard; but his companions greet his effort with approving shouts of "Yi! yi!" They look so fierce, and yet are so childishly happy, that at the thought of their exile and of the dark tenement the question arises, "Why all this joy?" The guide answers it with a look of surprise. "They sing," he says, "because they are glad they are free. Did you not know?"

The bells in old Trinity chime the midnight hour. From dark hallways men and women pour forth and hasten to the Maronite church. In the loft of the dingy old warehouse wax candles burn before an altar of brass. The priest, in a white robe with a huge gold cross worked on the back, chants the ritual. The people respond. The women kneel in the aisles, shrouding their heads in their shawls; the surpliced acolyte swings his censer; the heavy perfume of burning incense fills the hall.

The band at the anarchists' ball is tuning up for the last dance. Young and old float to the happy strains, forgetting injustice, oppression, hatred. Children slide upon the waxed floor, weaving fearlessly in and out between the couples—between fierce, bearded men and short-haired women with crimson-bordered kerchiefs. A Punch-and-Judy show in the corner evokes shouts of laughter.

Outside the snow is falling. It sifts silently into each nook and corner, softens all the hard and ugly lines, and throws the spotless mantle of charity over the blemishes, the shortcomings. Christmas morning will dawn pure and white.

'T WAS LIZA'S DOINGS

JOE drove his old gray mare along the stony road in deep thought. They had been across the ferry to Newtown with a load of Christmas truck. It had been a hard pull uphill for them both, for Joe had found it necessary not a few times to get down and give old 'Liza a lift to help her over the roughest spots; and now, going home, with the twilight coming on and no other job a-waiting, he let her have her own way. It was slow, but steady, and it suited Joe; for his head was full of busy thoughts, and there were few enough of them that were pleasant.

Business had been bad at the big stores, never worse, and what trucking there was there were too many about. Storekeepers who never used to look at a dollar, so long as they knew they could trust the man who did their

47

hauling, were counting the nickels these days. As for chance jobs like this one, that was all over now with the holidays, and there had been little enough of it, too.

There would be less, a good deal, with the hard winter at the door, and with 'Liza to keep and the many mouths to fill. Still, he would n't have minded it so much but for mother fretting and worrying herself sick at home, and all along o' Jim, the eldest boy, who had gone away mad and never come back. Many were the dollars he had paid the doctor and the druggist to fix her up, but it was no use. She was worrying herself into a decline, it was clear to be seen.

Joe heaved a heavy sigh as he thought of the strapping lad who had brought such sorrow to his mother. So strong and so handy on the wagon. Old 'Liza loved him like a brother and minded him even better than she did himself. If he only had him now, they could face the winter and the bad times, and pull through. But things never had gone right since he left. He did n't know, Joe thought humbly as he jogged along over the rough road, but he had been a little hard on the lad. Boys wanted a chance once in a while. All work and no play was not for

them. Likely he had forgotten he was a boy
once himself. But Jim was such a big lad,
'most like a man. He took after his mother
more than the rest. She had been proud, too,
when she was a girl. He wished he had n't
been hasty that time they had words about
those boxes at the store. Anyway, it turned
out that it was n't Jim's fault. But he was
gone that night, and try as they might to find
him, they never had word of him since. And
Joe sighed again more heavily than before.

Old 'Liza shied at something in the road,
and Joe took a firmer hold on the reins. It
turned his thoughts to the horse. She was
getting old, too, and not as handy as she was.
He noticed that she was getting winded with
a heavy load. It was well on to ten years she
had been their capital and the breadwinner of
the house. Sometimes he thought that she
missed Jim. If she was to leave them now, he
would n't know what to do, for he could n't
raise the money to buy another horse nohow,
as things were. Poor old 'Liza! He stroked
her gray coat musingly with the point of his
whip as he thought of their old friendship.
The horse pointed one ear back toward her
master and neighed gently, as if to assure him
that she was all right.

4

Suddenly she stumbled. Joe pulled her
up in time, and throwing the reins over her
back, got down to see what it was. An old
horseshoe, and in the dust beside it a new
silver quarter. He picked both up and put
the shoe in the wagon.

"They say it is luck," he mused, "finding
horse-iron and money. Maybe it's my Christmas. Get up, 'Liza!" And he drove off to
the ferry.

THE glare of a thousand gas-lamps had
chased the sunset out of the western sky,
when Joe drove home through the city's
streets. Between their straight mile-long
rows surged the busy life of the coming
holiday. In front of every grocery-store was
a grove of fragrant Christmas trees waiting
to be fitted into little green stands with fairy
fences. Within, customers were bargaining,
chatting, and bantering the busy clerks. Peddlers offering tinsel and colored candles way-
laid them on the door-step. The rack under
the butcher's awning fairly groaned with its
weight of plucked geese, of turkeys, stout and
skinny, of poultry of every kind. The saloon-
keeper even had wreathed his door-posts in
ground-ivy and hemlock, and hung a sprig

of holly in the window, as if with a spurious promise of peace on earth and good-will toward men who entered there. It tempted not Joe. He drove past it to the corner, where he turned up a street darker and lonelier than the rest, toward a stretch of rocky, vacant lots fenced in by an old stone wall. 'Liza turned in at the rude gate without being told, and pulled up at the house.

A plain little one-story frame with a lean-to for a kitchen, and an adjoining stable-shed, over-shadowed all by two great chestnuts of the days when there were country lanes where now are paved streets, and on Manhattan Island there was farm by farm. A light gleamed in the window looking toward the street. As 'Liza's hoofs were heard on the drive, a young girl with a shawl over her head ran out from some shelter where she had been watching, and took the reins from Joe.

"You're late," she said, stroking the mare's steaming flank. 'Liza reached around and rubbed her head against the girl's shoulder, nibbling playfully at the fringe of her shawl.

"Yes; we've come far, and it's been a hard pull. 'Liza is tired. Give her a good feed, and I'll bed her down. How's mother?"

"Sprier than she was," replied the girl,

bending over the shaft to unbuckle the horse;
"seems as if she 'd kinder cheered up for
Christmas." And she led 'Liza to the stable
while her father backed the wagon into the
shed.

It was warm and very comfortable in the
little kitchen, where he joined the family
after "washing up." The fire burned brightly
in the range, on which a good-sized roast
sizzled cheerily in its pot, sending up clouds
of savory steam. The sand on the white pine
floor was swept in tongues, old-country fashion. Joe and his wife were both born across
the sea, and liked to keep Christmas eve as
they had kept it when they were children.
Two little boys and a younger girl than the
one who had met him at the gate received him
with shouts of glee, and pulled him straight
from the door to look at a hemlock branch
stuck in the tub of sand in the corner. It
was their Christmas tree, and they were to
light it with candles, red and yellow and
green, which mama got them at the grocer's
where the big Santa Claus stood on the shelf.
They pranced about like so many little colts,
and clung to Joe by turns, shouting all at
once, each one anxious to tell the great news
first and loudest.

Joe took them on his knee, all three, and
when they had shouted until they had to stop
for breath, he pulled from under his coat a
paper bundle, at which the children's eyes
bulged. He undid the wrapping slowly.

"Who do you think has come home with
me?" he said, and he held up before them the
veritable Santa Claus himself, done in plaster
and all snow-covered. He had bought it at
the corner toy-store with his lucky quarter.
"I met him on the road over on Long Island,
where 'Liza and I was to-day, and I gave him
a ride to town. They say it 's luck falling
in with Santa Claus, partickler when there 's
a horseshoe along. I put hisn up in the barn,
in 'Liza's stall. Maybe our luck will turn
yet, eh! old woman?" And he put his arm
around his wife, who was setting out the
dinner with Jennie, and gave her a good
hug, while the children danced off with their
Santa Claus.

She was a comely little woman, and she
tried hard to be cheerful. She gave him a
brave look and a smile, but there were tears
in her eyes, and Joe saw them, though he let
on that he did n't. He patted her tenderly
on the back and smoothed his Jennie's yellow
braids, while he swallowed the lump in his

throat and got it down and out of the way.
He needed no doctor to tell him that Santa
Claus would not come again and find her cook-
ing their Christmas dinner, unless she mended
soon and swiftly.

They ate their dinner together, and sat and
talked until it was time to go to bed. Joe
went out to make all snug about 'Liza for the
night and to give her an extra feed. He
stopped in the door, coming back, to shake
the snow out of his clothes. It was coming
on with bad weather and a northerly storm,
he reported. The snow was falling thick
already and drifting badly. He saw to the
kitchen fire and put the children to bed.
Long before the clock in the neighboring
church-tower struck twelve, and its doors
were opened for the throngs come to worship
at the midnight mass, the lights in the cottage
were out, and all within it fast asleep.

THE murmur of the homeward-hurrying
crowds had died out, and the last echoing
shout of "Merry Christmas!" had been
whirled away on the storm, now grown fierce
with bitter cold, when a lonely wanderer came
down the street. It was a boy, big and strong-
limbed, and, judging from the manner in

which he pushed his way through the gathering drifts, not unused to battle with the world,
but evidently in hard luck. His jacket, white
with the falling snow, was scant and worn
nearly to rags, and there was that in his face
which spoke of hunger and suffering silently
endured. He stopped at the gate in the stone
fence, and looked long and steadily at the cottage in the chestnuts. No life stirred within,
and he walked through the gap with slow and
hesitating step. Under the kitchen window
he stood awhile, sheltered from the storm, as
if undecided, then stepped to the horse-shed
and rapped gently on the door.

"'Liza!" he called, "'Liza, old girl! It's
me—Jim!"

A low, delighted whinnying from the stall
told the shivering boy that he was not forgotten there. The faithful beast was straining at
her halter in a vain effort to get at her friend.
Jim raised a bar that held the door closed by
the aid of a lever within, of which he knew
the trick, and went in. The horse made room
for him in her stall, and laid her shaggy head
against his cheek.

"Poor old 'Liza!" he said, patting her neck
and smoothing her gray coat, "poor old girl!
Jim has one friend that has n't gone back on

him. I 've come to keep Christmas with you,
'Liza! Had your supper, eh? You 're in luck.
I have n't; I was n't bid, 'Liza; but never
mind. You shall feed for both of us. Here
goes!" He dug into the oats-bin with the
measure, and poured it full into 'Liza's crib.

"Fill up, old girl! and good night to you."
With a departing pat he crept up the ladder
to the loft above, and, scooping out a berth
in the loose hay, snuggled down in it to sleep.
Soon his regular breathing up there kept step
with the steady munching of the horse in her
stall. The two reunited friends were dreaming happy Christmas dreams.

The night wore into the small hours of
Christmas morning. The fury of the storm
was unabated. The old cottage shook under
the fierce blasts, and the chestnuts waved their
hoary branches wildly, beseechingly, above it,
as if they wanted to warn those within of
some threatened danger. But they slept and
heard them not. From the kitchen chimney,
after a blast more violent than any that had
gone before, a red spark issued, was whirled
upward and beaten against the shingle roof
of the barn, swept clean of snow. Another
followed it, and another. Still they slept in
the cottage; the chestnuts moaned and bran-

dished their arms in vain. The storm fanned one of the sparks into a flame. It flickered for a moment and then went out. So, at least, it seemed. But presently it reappeared, and with it a faint glow was reflected in the attic window over the door. Down in her stall 'Liza moved uneasily. Nobody responding, she plunged and reared, neighing loudly for help. The storm drowned her calls; her master slept, unheeding.

But one heard it, and in the nick of time. The door of the shed was thrown violently open, and out plunged Jim, his hair on fire and his clothes singed and smoking. He brushed the sparks off himself as if they were flakes of snow. Quick as thought, he tore 'Liza's halter from its fastening, pulling out staple and all, threw his smoking coat over her eyes, and backed her out of the shed. He reached in, and pulling the harness off the hook, threw it as far into the snow as he could, yelling "Fire!" at the top of his voice. Then he jumped on the back of the horse, and beating her with heels and hands into a mad gallop, was off up the street before the bewildered inmates of the cottage had rubbed the sleep out of their eyes and come out to see the barn on fire and burning up.

Down street and avenue fire-engines raced with clanging bells, leaving tracks of glowing coals in the snow-drifts, to the cottage in the chestnut lots. They got there just in time to see the roof crash into the barn, burying, as Joe and his crying wife and children thought, 'Liza and their last hope in the fiery wreck. The door had blown shut, and the harness Jim threw out was snowed under. No one dreamed that the mare was not there. The flames burst through the wreck and lit up the cottage and swaying chestnuts. Joe and his family stood in the shelter of it, looking sadly on. For the second time that Christmas night tears came into the honest truckman's eyes. He wiped them away with his cap.

"Poor 'Liza!" he said.

A hand was laid with gentle touch upon his arm. He looked up. It was his wife. Her face beamed with a great happiness.

"Joe," she said, "you remember what you read: 'tidings of great joy.' Oh, Joe, Jim has come home!"

She stepped aside, and there was Jim, sister Jennie hanging on his neck, and 'Liza alive and neighing her pleasure. The lad looked at his father and hung his head.

"Jim saved her, father," said Jennie, patting the gray mare; "it was him fetched the engine."

Joe took a step toward his son and held out his hand to him.

"Jim," he said, "you 're a better man nor yer father. From now on, you 'n' I run the truck on shares. But mind this, Jim: never leave mother no more."

And in the clasp of the two hands all the past was forgotten and forgiven. Father and son had found each other again.

"'Liza," said the truckman, with sudden vehemence, turning to the old mare and putting his arm around her neck, "'Liza! It was your doin's. I knew it was luck when I found them things. Merry Christmas!" And he kissed her smack on her hairy mouth, one, two, three times.

THE DUBOURQUES, FATHER
AND SON

IT must be nearly a quarter of a century since I first met the Dubourques. There are plenty of old New-Yorkers yet who will recall them as I saw them, plodding along Chatham street, swarthy, silent, meanly dressed, undersized, with their great tin signs covering front and back, like ill-favored gnomes turned sandwich-men to vent their spite against a gay world. Sunshine or rain, they went their way, Indian file, never apart, bearing their everlasting, unavailing protest.

"I demand," read the painted signs, "the will and testament of my brother, who died in California, leaving a large property inheritance to Virgile Dubourque, which has never reached him."

That was all any one was ever able to make

out. At that point the story became rambling
and unintelligible. Denunciation, hot and
wrathful, of the thieves, whoever they were,
of the government, of bishops, priests, and
lawyers, alternated with protestations of in-
nocence of heaven knows what crimes. If any
one stopped them to ask what it was all
about, they stared, shook their heads, and
passed on. If money was offered, they took it
without thanking the giver; indeed, without
noticing him. They were never seen apart,
yet never together in the sense of being apparently anything to each other. I doubt if
they ever spoke, unless they were obliged to.
Grim and lonely, they traveled the streets,
parading their grievance before an unheeding day.

What that grievance was, and what was
their story, a whole generation had tried
vainly to find out. Every young reporter
tried his hand at it at least once, some many
times, I among them. None of us ever found
out anything tangible about them. Now and
then we ran down a rumor in the region of
Bleecker street, then the "French quarter,"
—I should have said that they were French
and spoke but a few words of broken English
when they spoke at all,—only to have it come

to nothing. One which I recall was to the effect that, at some time in the far past, the elder of the two had been a schoolmaster in Lorraine, and had come across the sea in quest of a fabulous fortune left by his brother, one of the gold-diggers of '49, who died in his boots; that there had been some disagreement between father and son, which resulted in the latter running away with their saved-up capital, leaving the old man stranded in a strange city, among people of strange speech, without the means of asserting his claim, and that, when he realized this, he lost his reason. Thus his son, Erneste, found him, returning after years penniless and repentant.

From that meeting father and son came forth what they were ever since. So ran the story, but whether it was all fancy, or some or most of it, I could not tell. No one could. One by one, the reporters dropped them, unable to make them out. The officers of a French benevolent society, where twice a week they received fixed rations, gave up importuning them to accept the shelter of the house before their persistent, almost fierce, refusal. The police did not trouble them, except when people complained that the tin signs tore their clothes. After that they walked with canvas posters, and were let alone.

One morning in the winter of 1882, among the police reports of the night's happenings that were laid upon my desk, I found one saying that Virgile Dubourque, Frenchman, seventy-five years old, had died in a Wooster-street lodging-house. The story of his death, as I learned it there that day, was as tragic as that of his life. He had grown more and more feeble, until at last he was unable to leave the house. For the first time the son went out alone. The old man sat by the stove all day, silently brooding over his wrongs. The lodgers came and went. He heeded neither their going nor their coming. Through the long night he kept his seat, gazing fixedly into the fire. In the morning, when daylight shone upon the cold, gray ashes, he sat there dead. The son slept peacefully beside him.

The old schoolmaster took his last trip alone; no mourners rode behind the hearse to the Palisade Cemetery, where charitable countrymen bought him a grave. Erneste did not go to the funeral. That afternoon I met him on Broadway, plodding alone over the old route. His eyes were red and swollen.

The "protest" hung from his shoulders; in his hand he carried, done up roughly in a pack, the signs the old man had borne. A look of such utter loneliness as I had never seen on a human face came into his when I asked him where his father was. He made a gesture of dejection and shifted his feet uneasily, as if impatient at being detained. Something distracted my attention for the moment, and when I looked again he was gone.

Once in the following summer I heard from Erneste through the newspapers, just when I had begun to miss him from his old haunts. It seems that he had somehow found the papers that proved his claim, or thought he had. He had put them into the hands of the French consul the day before, said the item, appearing before him clothed and in his right mind, without the signs. But the account merely added to the mystery by hinting that the old man had unconsciously hoarded the papers all the years he sought them with such toil in the streets of New York. Here was my story at last; but before I could lay hold of it, it evaded me once more in the hurry and worry of the police office.

Autumn had come and nearly gone, when

New York was one day startled by the report
that a madman had run through Fourteenth
street at an hour in the afternoon when it
was most crowded with shoppers, and, with
a pair of carpenter's compasses, had cut
right and left, stabbing as many as came in
his way. A scene of the wildest panic en-
sued. Women flung themselves down base-
ment-steps and fell fainting in doorways.
Fully half a score were cut down, among
them the wife of Policeman Hanley, who was
on duty in the block, and who arrested the
maniac without knowing that his wife lay
mortally wounded among his victims. She
had come out to meet him, with the children.
It was only after he had attended to the rest
and sent the prisoner away securely bound
that he was told there was still a wounded
woman in the next store, and found her there
with her little ones.

The madman was Erneste Dubourque. I
found him in the police station, surrounded
by a crowd of excited officials, to whose inquiries he turned a mien of dull and stolid
indifference. He knew me when I called him
by name, and looked up with a movement of
quick intelligence, as one who suddenly remembers something he had forgotten and

5

vainly tried to recall. He started for the
door. When they seized him and brought
him back, he fought like a demon. His
shrieks of "Thieves! robbers!" filled the
building as they bore him struggling to a
cell.

He was tried by a jury and acquitted of
murder. The defense was insanity. The
court ordered his incarceration in a safe asylum. The police had received a severe lesson,
and during the next month, while it was yet
fresh in the public mind, they bestirred themselves, and sent a number of "harmless"
lunatics, who had gone about unmolested,
after him. I never heard of Erneste Dubourque again; but even now, after fifteen
years, I find myself sometimes asking the
old question: What was the story of wrong
that bore such a crop of sorrow and darkness and murder?

ABE'S GAME OF JACKS

TIME hung heavily on Abe Seelig's hands, alone, or as good as alone, in the flat on the "stoop" of the Allen-street tenement. His mother had gone to the butcher's. Chajim, the father,—"Chajim" is the Yiddish of "Herman,"—was long at the shop. To Abe was committed the care of his two young brothers, Isaac and Jacob. Abraham was nine, and past time for fooling. Play is "fooling" in the sweaters' tenements, and the muddling of ideas makes trouble, later on, to which the police returns have the index.

"Don't let 'em on the stairs," the mother had said, on going, with a warning nod toward the bed where Jake and Ikey slept. He did n't intend to. Besides, they were fast asleep. Abe cast about him for fun of some kind, and bethought himself of a game of jacks.

That he had no jackstones was of small moment to him.   East-Side tenements, where
pennies are infrequent, have resources.   One
penny was Abe's hoard.   With that, and an
accidental match, he began the game.

It went on well enough, albeit slightly lop-
sided by reason of the penny being so much
the weightier, until the match, in one unlucky
throw, fell close to a chair by the bed, and,
in falling, caught fire.

Something hung down from the chair, and
while Abe gazed, open-mouthed, at the match,
at the chair, and at the bed right alongside,
with his sleeping brothers on it, the little
blaze caught it.   The flame climbed up, up,
up, and a great smoke curled under the ceiling.   The children still slept, locked in each
other's arms, and Abe—Abe ran.

He ran, frightened half out of his senses,
out of the room, out of the house, into the
street, to the nearest friendly place he knew,
a grocery-store five doors away, where his
mother traded; but she was not there.   Abe
merely saw that she was not there, then he
hid himself trembling.

In all the block, where three thousand tenants live, no one knew what cruel thing was
happening on the stoop of No. 19.

A train passed on the elevated road, slowing up for the station near by. The engineer saw one wild whirl of fire within the room, and opening the throttle of his whistle wide, let out a screech so long and so loud that in ten seconds the street was black with men and women rushing out to see what dreadful thing had happened.

No need of asking. From the door of the Seelig flat, burned through, fierce flames reached across the hall, barring the way. The tenement was shut in.

Promptly it poured itself forth upon fire-escape ladders, front and rear, with shrieks and wailing. In the street the crowd became a deadly crush. Police and firemen battered their way through, ran down and over men, women, and children, with a desperate effort.

The firemen from Hook and Ladder Six, around the corner, had heard the shrieks, and, knowing what they portended, ran with haste. But they were too late with their extinguishers; could not even approach the burning flat. They could only throw up their ladders to those above. For the rest they must needs wait until the engines came.

One tore up the street, coupled on a hose, and ran it into the house. Then died out the fire in the flat as speedily as it had come. The burning room was pumped full of water, and the firemen entered.

Just within the room they came upon little Jacob, still alive, but half roasted. He had struggled from the bed nearly to the door. On the bed lay the body of Isaac, the youngest, burned to a crisp.

They carried Jacob to the police station. As they brought him out, a frantic woman burst through the throng and threw herself upon him. It was the children's mother come back. When they took her to the blackened corpse of little Ike, she went stark mad. A dozen neighbors held her down, shrieking, while others went in search of the father.

In the street the excitement grew until it became almost uncontrollable when the dead boy was carried out.

In the midst of it little Abe returned, pale, silent, and frightened, to stand by his raving mother.

A LITTLE PICTURE

THE fire-bells rang on the Bowery in the small hours of the morning. One of the old dwelling-houses that remain from the day when the "Bouwerie" was yet remembered as an avenue of beer-gardens and pleasure resorts was burning. Down in the street stormed the firemen, coupling hose and dragging it to the front. Up-stairs in the peak of the roof, in the broken skylight, hung a man, old, feeble, and gasping for breath, struggling vainly to get out. He had piled chairs upon tables, and climbed up where he could grasp the edge, but his strength had given out when one more effort would have freed him. He felt himself sinking back. Over him was the sky, reddened now by the fire that raged below. Through the hole the pent-up smoke in the

71

building found vent and rushed in a black and stifling cloud.

" Air, air ! " gasped the old man. " O God, water ! "

There was a swishing sound, a splash, and the copious spray of a stream sent over the house from the street fell upon his upturned face. It beat back the smoke. Strength and hope returned. He took another grip on the rafter just as he would have let go.

" Oh, that I might be reached yet and saved from this awful death ! " he prayed. " Help, O God, help ! "

An answering cry came over the adjoining roof. He had been heard, and the firemen, who did not dream that any one was in the burning building, had him in a minute. He had been asleep in the store when the fire aroused him and drove him, blinded and bewildered, to the attic, where he was trapped.

Safe in the street, the old man fell upon his knees.

" I prayed for water, and it came; I prayed for freedom, and was saved. The God of my fathers be praised ! " he said, and bowed his head in thanksgiving.

A DREAM OF THE WOODS

SOMETHING came over Police Headquarters in the middle of the summer night. It was like the sighing of the north wind in the branches of the tall firs and in the reeds along lonely river-banks where the otter dips from the brink for its prey. The doorman, who yawned in the hall, and to whom reed-grown river-banks have been strangers so long that he has forgotten they ever were, shivered and thought of pneumonia.

The sergeant behind the desk shouted for some one to close the door; it was getting as cold as January. The little messenger boy on the lowest step of the oaken stairs nodded and dreamed in his sleep of Uncas and Chingachgook and the great woods. The cunning old beaver was there in his hut, and he heard the crack of Deerslayer's rifle.

He knew all the time he was dreaming, sitting on the steps of Police Headquarters, and yet it was all as real to him as if he were there, with the Mingoes creeping up to him in ambush all about and reaching for his scalp.

While he slept, a light step had passed, and the moccasin of the woods left its trail in his dream. In with the gust through the Mulberry-street door had come a strange pair, an old woman and a bright-eyed child, led by a policeman, and had passed up to Matron Travers's quarters on the top floor.

Strangely different, they were yet alike, both children of the woods. The woman was a squaw typical in looks and bearing, with the straight black hair, dark skin, and stolid look of her race. She climbed the steps wearily, holding the child by the hand. The little one skipped eagerly, two steps at a time. There was the faintest tinge of brown in her plump cheeks, and a roguish smile in the corner of her eyes that made it a hardship not to take her up in one's lap and hug her at sight. In her frock of red-and-white calico she was a fresh and charming picture, with all the grace of movement and the sweet shyness of a young fawn.

The policeman had found them sitting on a

big trunk in the Grand Central Station, waiting patiently for something or somebody that
did n't come. When he had let them sit until
he thought the child ought to be in bed, he
took them into the police station in the depot,
and there an effort was made to find out who
and what they were. It was not an easy matter. Neither could speak English. They knew
a few words of French, however, and between
that and a note the old woman had in her
pocket the general outline of the trouble was
gathered. They were of the Canaghwaga tribe
of Iroquois, domiciled in the St. Regis reservation across the Canadian border, and had
come down to sell a trunkful of beads, and
things worked with beads. Some one was to
meet them, but had failed to come, and these
two, to whom the trackless wilderness was
as an open book, were lost in the city of ten
thousand homes. .

The matron made them understand by signs
that two of the nine white beds in the nursery were for them, and they turned right in,
humbly and silently thankful. The little girl
had carried up with her, hugged very close
under her arm, a doll that was a real ethno-
logical study. It was a faithful rendering of
the Indian papoose, whittled out of a chunk

of wood, with two staring glass beads for eyes, and strapped to a board the way Indian babies are, under a coverlet of very gaudy blue. It was a marvelous doll baby, and its nurse was mighty proud of it. She did n't let it go when she went to bed. It slept with her, and got up to play with her as soon as the first ray of daylight peeped in over the tall roofs.

The morning brought visitors, who admired the doll, chirruped to the little girl, and tried to talk with her grandmother, for that they made her out to be. To most questions she simply answered by shaking her head and holding out her credentials. There were two letters: one to the conductor of the train from Montreal, asking him to see that they got through all right; the other, a memorandum, for her own benefit apparently, recounting the number of hearts, crosses, and other treasures she had in her trunk. It was from those she had left behind at the reservation.

"Little Angus," it ran, "sends what is over to sell for him. Sarah sends the hearts. As soon as you can, will you try and sell some hearts?" Then there was "love to mother," and lastly an account of what the mason had said about the chimney of the cabin. They had sent for him to fix it. It was very dan-

gerous the way it was, ran the message, and
if mother would get the bricks, he would fix
it right away.

The old squaw looked on with an anxious
expression while the note was being read, as
if she expected some sense to come out of it
that would find her folks; but none of that
kind could be made out of it, so they sat and
waited until General Parker should come in.

General Ely S. Parker was the "big Indian" of Mulberry street in a very real sense.
Though he was a clerk in the Police Department and never went on the war-path any
more, he was the head of the ancient Indian
Confederacy, chief of the Six Nations, once so
powerful for mischief, and now a mere name
that frightens no one. Donegahawa—one
cannot help wishing that the picturesque old
chief had kept his name of the council lodge
—was not born to sit writing at an office desk.
In youth he tracked the bear and the panther
in the Northern woods. The scattered remnants of the tribes East and West owned his
rightful authority as chief. The Canaghwa-
gas were one of these. So these lost ones had
come straight to the official and actual head
of their people when they were stranded in
the great city. They knew it when they

heard the magic name of Donegahawa, and
sat silently waiting and wondering till he
should come. The child looked up admiringly
at the gold-laced cap of Inspector Williams,
when he took her on his knee, and the stern
face of the big policeman relaxed and grew
tender as a woman's as he took her face between his hands and kissed it.

When the general came in, he spoke to
them at once in their own tongue, and very
sweet and musical it was. Then their troubles were soon over. The sachem, when he
had heard their woes, said two words between puffs of his pipe that cleared all the
shadows away. They sounded to the pale-
face ear like " Huh Hoo—ochsjawai," or something equally barbarous, but they meant that
there were not so many Indians in town but
that theirs could be found, and in that the
sachem was right. The number of redskins
in Thompson street—they all live over there—
is about seven.

The old squaw, when she was told that her
friend would be found, got up promptly, and,
ᵗing first to Inspector Williams and the
er officials in the room, and next to the
ₑeneral, said very sweetly, "Njeawa," and
Lightfoot—that was the child's name, it ap-

peared—said it after her; which meant, the general explained, that they were very much obliged. Then they went out in charge of a policeman, to begin their search, little Lightfoot hugging her doll and looking back over her shoulder at the many gold-laced policemen who had captured her little heart. And they kissed their hands after her.

Mulberry street awoke from its dream of youth, of the fields and the deep woods, to the knowledge that it was a bad day. The old doorman, who had stood at the gate patiently answering questions for twenty years, told the first man who came looking for a lost child, with sudden resentment, that he ought to be locked up for losing her, and, pushing him out in the rain, slammed the door after him.

A HEATHEN BABY

A STACK of mail comes to Police Headquarters every morning from the precincts by special department carrier. It in-
cludes the reports for the last twenty-four
hours of stolen and recovered goods, com-
plaints, and the thousand and one things the
official mail-bag contains from day to day. It
is all routine, and everything has its own
pigeonhole into which it drops and is forgotten until some raking up in the department turns up the old blotters and the old
things once more. But at last the mail-bag
contained something that was altogether out
of the usual run, to wit, a Chinese baby.

Piccaninnies have come in it before this,
lots of them, black and shiny, and one papoose from a West-Side wigwam; but a Chinese baby never.

Sergeant Jack was so astonished that it took his breath away. When he recovered he spoke learnedly about its clothes as evidence of its heathen origin. Never saw such a thing before, he said. They were like they were sewn on; it was impossible to disentangle that child by any way short of rolling it on the floor.

Sergeant Jack is an old bachelor, and that is all he knows about babies. The child was not sewn up at all. It was just swaddled, and no Chinese had done that, but the Italian woman who found it. Sergeant Jack sees such babies every night in Mulberry street, but that is the way with old bachelors. They don't know much, anyhow.

It was clear that the baby thought so. She was a little girl, very little, only one night old; and she regarded him through her almond eyes with a supercilious look, as who should say, "Now, if he was only a bottle, instead of a big, useless policeman, why, one might put up with him"; which reflection opened the flood-gates of grief and set the little Chinee squalling: "Yow! Yow! Yap!" until the sergeant held his ears, and a policeman carried it up-stairs in a hurry.

Down-stairs first, in the sergeant's big blot-

6

ter, and up-stairs in the matron's nursery
next, the baby's brief official history was recorded. There was very little of it, indeed,
and what there was was not marked by much
ceremony. The stork had n't brought it, as
it does in far-off Denmark; nor had the doctor found it and brought it in, on the American plan.

An Italian woman had just scratched it
out of an ash-barrel. Perhaps that 's the way
they find babies in China, in which case the
sympathy of all American mothers and fathers
will be with the present despoilers of the
heathen Chinee, who is entitled to no consid-
eration whatever until he introduces a new
way.

The Italian woman was Mrs. Maria Lepanto. She lives in Thompson street, but she
had come all the way down to the corner of
Elizabeth and Canal streets with her little
girl to look at a procession passing by. That
as everybody knows, is next door to China-
town. It was ten o'clock, and the end of the
procession was in sight, when she noticed
something stirring in an ash-barrel that stood
against the wall. She thought first it was a
rat, and was going to run, when a noise that
was certainly not a rat's squeal came from

the barrel. The child clung to her hand and dragged her toward the sound.

"Oh, mama!" she cried, in wild excitement, "hear it! It is n't a rat! I know! Hear!"

It was a wail, a very tiny wail, ever so sorry, as well it might be, coming from a baby that was cradled in an ash-barrel. It was little Susie's eager hands that snatched it out. Then they saw that it was indeed a child, a poor, helpless, grieving little baby.

It had nothing on at all, not even a rag. Perhaps they had not had time to dress it.

"Oh, it will fit my dolly's jacket!" cried Susie, dancing around and hugging it in glee. "It will, mama! A real live baby! Now Tilde need n't brag of theirs. We will take it home, won't we, mama?"

The bands brayed, and the flickering light of many torches filled the night. The procession had gone down the street, and the crowd with it. The poor woman wrapped the baby in her worn shawl and gave it to the girl to carry. And Susie carried it, prouder and happier than any of the men that marched to the music. So they arrived home. The little stranger had found friends and a resting-place.

But not for long. In the morning Mrs. Lepanto took counsel with the neighbors, and was told that the child must be given to the police. That was the law, they said, and though little Susie cried bitterly at having to part with her splendid new toy, Mrs. Lepanto, being a law-abiding woman, wrapped up her find and took it to the Macdougal-street station.

That was the way it got to Headquarters with the morning mail, and how Sergeant Jack got a chance to tell all he did n't know about babies. Matron Travers knew more, a good deal. She tucked the little heathen away in a trundle-bed with a big bottle, and blessed silence fell at once on Headquarters. In five minutes the child was asleep.

While it slept, Matron Travers entered it in her book as "No. 103" of that year's crop of the gutter, and before it woke up she was on the way with it, snuggled safely in a big gray shawl, up to the Charities. There Mr. Bauer registered it under yet another number, chucked it under the chin, and chirped at it in what he probably thought might pass for baby Chinese. Then it got another big bottle and went to sleep once more.

At ten o'clock there came a big ship on purpose to give the little Mott-street waif a ride up the river, and by dinner-time it was on a green island with four hundred other babies of all kinds and shades, but not one just like it in the whole lot. For it was New York's first and only Chinese foundling. As to that Superintendent Bauer, Matron Travers, and Mrs. Lepanto agreed. Sergeant Jack's evidence does n't count, except as backed by his superiors. He does n't know a heathen baby when he sees one.

The island where the waif from Mott street cast anchor is called Randall's Island, and there its stay ends, or begins. The chances are that it ends, for with an ash-barrel filling its past and a foundling asylum its future, a baby has n't much of a show. Babies were made to be hugged each by one pair of mother's arms, and neither white-capped nurses nor sleek milch-cows fed on the fattest of meadow-grass can take their place, try as they may. The babies know that they are cheated, and they will not stay.

HE KEPT HIS TRYST

POLICEMAN SCHULTZ was stamping up and down his beat in Hester street, trying to keep warm, on the night before Christmas, when a human wreck, in rum and rags, shuffled across his path and hailed him:

"You allus treated me fair, Schultz," it said; "say, will you do a thing for me?"

"What is it, Denny?" said the officer. He had recognized the wreck as Denny the Robber, a tramp who had haunted his beat ever since he had been on it, and for years before, he had heard, further back than any one knew.

"Will you," said the wreck, wistfully—"will you run me in and give me about three months to-morrow? Will you do it?"

"That I will," said Schultz. He had often done it before, sometimes for three, sometimes

86

for six months, and sometimes for ten days,
according to how he and Denny and the justice
felt about it.   In the spell between trips to
the island, Denny was a regular pensioner of
the policeman, who let him have a quarter or
so when he had so little money as to be next
to desperate.   He never did get quite to that
point. Perhaps the policeman's quarters saved
him.   His nickname of "the Robber" was
given to him on the same principle that
dubbed the neighborhood he haunted the Pig
Market—because pigs are the only ware not
for sale there.   Denny never robbed anybody.   The only thing he ever stole was the
time he should have spent in working. There
was no denying it, Denny was a loafer.   He
himself had told Schultz that it was because
his wife and children put him out of their
house in Madison street five years before.
Perhaps if his wife's story had been heard it
would have reversed that statement of facts.
But nobody ever heard it.   Nobody took the
trouble to inquire.   The O'Neil family—that
was understood to be the name—interested
no one in Jewtown.   One of its members
was enough.   Except that Mrs. O'Neil lived
in Madison street, somewhere "near Lundy's
store," nothing was known of her.

"That I will, Denny," repeated the policeman, heartily, slipping him a dime for luck.
"You come around to-morrow, and I will run
you in. Now go along."

But Denny did n't go, though he had the
price of two "balls" at the distillery. He
shifted thoughtfully on his feet, and said:

"Say, Schultz, if I should die now,—I am
all full o' rheumatiz, and sore,—if I should
die before, would you see to me and tell the
wife?"

"Small fear of yer dying, Denny, with the
price of two drinks," said the policeman, poking him facetiously in the ribs with his club.
"Don't you worry. All the same, if you will
tell me where the old woman lives, I will let
her know. What's the number?"

But the Robber's mood had changed under
the touch of the silver dime that burned his
palm. "Never mind, Schultz," he said; "I
guess I won't kick; so long!" and moved off.

THE snow drifted wickedly down Suffolk
street Christmas morning, pinching noses and
ears and cheeks already pinched by hunger
and want. It set around the corner into the
Pig Market, where the hucksters plodded
knee-deep in the drifts, burying the horse-

radish man and his machine, and coating the bare, plucked breasts of the geese that swung from countless hooks at the corner stand with softer and whiter down than ever grew there. It drove the suspender-man into the hallway of a Suffolk-street tenement, where he tried to pluck the icicles from his frozen ears and beard with numb and powerless fingers.

As he stepped out of the way of some one entering with a blast that set like a cold shiver up through the house, he stumbled over something, and put down his hand to feel what it was. It touched a cold face, and the house rang with a shriek that silenced the clink of glasses in the distillery, against the side door of which the something lay. They crowded out, glasses in hand, to see what it was.

"Only a dead tramp," said some one, and the crowd went back to the warm saloon, where the barrels lay in rows on the racks. The clink of glasses and shouts of laughter came through the peep-hole in the door into the dark hallway as Policeman Schultz bent over the stiff, cold shape. Some one had called him.

"Denny," he said, tugging at his sleeve.

"Denny, come. Your time is up. I am here."
Denny never stirred. The policeman looked
up, white in the face.

"My God!" he said, "he's dead. But he
kept his date."

And so he had. Denny the Robber was
dead. Rum and exposure and the "rheumatiz" had killed him. Policeman Schultz
kept his word, too, and had him taken to
the station on a stretcher.

"He was a bad penny," said the saloon-
keeper, and no one in Jewtown was found to
contradict him.

JOHN GAVIN, MISFIT

JOHN GAVIN was to blame—there is no doubt of that. To be sure, he was out of a job, with never a cent in his pockets, his babies starving, and notice served by the landlord that day. He had traveled the streets till midnight looking for work, and had found none. And so he gave up. Gave up, with the Employment Bureau in the next street registering applicants; with the Way-farers' Lodge over in Poverty Gap, where he might have earned fifty cents, anyway, chopping wood; with charities without end, organized and unorganized, that would have referred his case, had they done nothing else. With all these things and a hundred like them to meet their wants, the Gavins of our day have been told often enough that they have no business to lose hope. That they will persist is strange. But perhaps this one had never heard of them.

Anyway, Gavin is dead. But yesterday he was the father of six children, running from May, the eldest, who was thirteen and at school, to the baby, just old enough to poke its little fingers into its father's eyes and crow and jump when he came in from his long and dreary tramps. They were as happy a little family as a family of eight could be with the wolf scratching at the door, its nose already poking through. There had been no work and no wages in the house for months, and the landlord had given notice that at the end of the week out they must go, unless the back rent was paid. And there was about as much likelihood of its being paid as of a slice of the February sun dropping down through the ceiling into the room to warm the shivering Gavin family.

It began when Gavin's health gave way. He was a lather and had a steady job till sickness came. It was the old story: nothing laid away—how could there be, with a houseful of children?—and nothing coming in. They talk of death-rates to measure the misery of the slum by, but death does not touch the bottom. It ends the misery. Sickness only begins it. It began Gavin's. When he had to drop hammer and nails, he got a job in a saloon as a barkeeper; but the saloon did n't prosper, and when it was shut up, there was an end. Gavin did n't know it then. He looked at the babies and kept up spirits as well as he could, though it wrung his heart.

He tried everything under the sun to get a job. He traveled early and traveled late, but wherever he went they had men and to spare. And besides, he was ill. As they told him bluntly, sometimes, they did n't have any use for sick men. Men to work and earn wages must be strong. And he had to own that it was true.

Gavin was not strong. As he denied himself secretly the nourishment he needed that his little ones might have enough, he felt it more and more. It was harder work for him to get around, and each refusal left him more downcast. He was yet a young man, only thirty-four, but he felt as if he was old and tired—tired out; that was it.

The feeling grew on him while he went his last errand, offering his services at saloons and wherever, as he thought, an opening offered. In fact, he thought but little about it any more. The whole thing had become an empty, hopeless formality with him. He knew at last that he was looking for the thing he would never find; that in a cityful where every man had his place he was a misfit with none. With his dull brain dimly conscious of that one idea, he plodded homeward in the midnight hour. He had been on the go since early morning, and excepting some lunch from the saloon counters, had eaten nothing.

The lamp burned dimly in the room where May sat poring yet over her books, waiting for papa. When he came in she looked up and smiled, but saw by his look, as he hung up his hat, that there was no good news, and returned with a sigh to her book. The tired mother was asleep on the bed, dressed, with the baby in her arms. She had lain down to quiet it and had been lulled to sleep with it herself.

Gavin did not wake them. He went to the bed where the four little ones slept, and kissed them, each in his turn, then came back and kissed his wife and baby.

May nestled close to him as he bent over her and gave her, too, a little hug.

"Where are you going, papa?" she asked.

He turned around at the door and cast a look back at the quiet room, irresolute. Then he went back once more to kiss his sleeping wife and baby softly.

But however softly, it woke the mother. She saw him making for the door, and asked him where he meant to go so late.

"Out, just a little while," he said, and his voice was husky. He turned his head away.

A woman's instinct made her arise hastily and go to him.

"Don't go," she said; "please don't go away."

As he still moved toward the door, she put her arm about his neck and drew his head toward her.

She strove with him anxiously, frightened, she hardly knew herself by what. The lamp-light fell upon something shining which he held behind his back. The room rang with the shot, and the baby awoke crying, to see its father slip from mama's arms to the floor, dead.

For John Gavin, alive, there was no place. At least he did not find it; for which, let it be said and done with, he was to blame. Dead, society will find one for him. And for the one misfit got off the list there are seven whom not employment bureau nor woodyard nor charity register can be made to reach. Social economy the thing is called; which makes the eighth misfit.

IN THE CHILDREN'S HOSPITAL

THE fact was printed the other day that the half-hundred children or more who are in the hospitals on North Brother Island had no playthings, not even a rattle, to make the long days skip by, which, set in smallpox, scarlet fever, and measles, must be longer there than anywhere else in the world. The toys that were brought over there with a consignment of nursery tots who had the typhus fever had been worn clean out, except some fish-horns which the doctor frowned on, and which were therefore not allowed at large. Not as much as a red monkey on a yellow stick was there left on the island to make the youngsters happy.

That afternoon a big, hearty-looking man came into the office with the paper in his hand, and demanded to see the editor. He had come, he said, to see to it that those sick youngsters got the playthings they were entitled to ; and a regular Santa Claus he proved to the friend-less little colony on the lonely island, for he left a crisp fifty-dollar note behind when he went away without giving his name. The sin-gle condition was attached to the gift that it should be spent buying toys for the children on North Brother Island.

Accordingly, a strange invading army took the island by storm three or four nights ago. Under cover of the darkness it had itself ferried over from One Hundred and Thirty-eighth street in the department yawl, and be-fore morning it was in undisputed possession. It has come to stay. Not a doll or a sheep will ever leave the island again. They may riot upon it as they please, within certain well-defined limits, but none of them can ever cross the channel to the mainland again, un-less it be the rubber dolls who can swim, so it is said. Here is the muster-roll :

Six sheep (four with lambs), six fairies (big dolls in street-dress), twelve rubber dolls (in woolen jackets), four railroad-trains, twenty-eight base-balls, twenty rubber balls, six big painted (Scotch plaid) rubber balls, six still bigger ditto, seven boxes of blocks, half a dozen music-boxes, twenty-four rattles, six

7

bubble (soap) toys, twelve small engines, six games of dominoes, twelve rubber toys (old woman who lived in a shoe, etc.), five wooden toys (bad bear, etc.), thirty-six horse-reins.

As there is only one horse on the island, and that one a very steady-going steed in no urgent need of restraint, this last item might seem superfluous, but only to the uninstructed mind. Within a brief week half the boys and girls on the island that are out of bed long enough to stand on their feet will be transformed into ponies and the other half into drivers, and flying teams will go cavorting around to the tune of "Johnny, Get your Gun," and the "Jolly Brothers Gallop," as they are ground out of the music-boxes by little fingers that but just now toyed feebly with the balusters on the golden stair.

That music! When I went over to the island it fell upon my ears in little drops of sweet melody, as soon as I came in sight of the nurses' quarters. I listened, but could n't make out the tune. The drops seemed mixed. When I opened the door upon one of the nurses, Dr. Dixon, and the hospital matron, each grinding his or her music for all there was in it, and looking perfectly happy withal, I understood why.

They were all playing different tunes at the same time, the nurse "When the Robins Nest Again," Dr. Dixon "Nancy Lee," and the visitor "Sweet Violets." A little child stood by in open-mouthed admiration, that became ecstasy when I joined in with "The Babies on our Block." It was all for the little one's benefit, and she thought it beautiful without a doubt.

The storekeeper, knowing that music hath charms to soothe the breast of even a typhus-fever patient, had thrown in a dozen as his own gift. Thus one good deed brings on another, and a good deal more than fifty dollars' worth of happiness will be ground out on the island before there is an end of the music.

There is one little girl in the measles ward already who will eat only when her nurse sits by grinding out "Nancy Lee." She cannot be made to swallow one mouthful on any other condition. No other nurse and no other tune but "Nancy Lee" will do—neither the "Star-Spangled Banner" nor "The Babies on our Block." Whether it is Nancy all by her melodious self, or the beautiful picture of her in a sailor's suit on the lid of the box, or the two and the nurse and the dinner together, that serve to soothe her, is a question of some concern to the island, since Nancy and the nurse have shown signs of giving out together.

Three of the six sheep that were bought for the ridiculously low price of eighty-nine cents apiece, the lambs being thrown in as make-weight, were grazing on the mixed-measles lawn over on the east shore of the island, with a fairy in evening dress eying them rather disdainfully in the grasp of tearful Annie Cullum. Annie is a foundling from the asylum temporarily sojourning here. The measles and the scarlet fever were the only things that ever took kindly to her in her little life. They tackled her both at once, and poor Annie, after a six or eight weeks' tussle with them, has just about enough spunk left to cry when anybody looks at her.

Three woolly sheep and a fairy all at once have robbed her of all hope, and in the midst of it all she weeps as if her heart would break. Even when the nurse pulls one of the unresisting mutton heads, and it emits a loud "Baa-a," she stops only just for a second or two and then wails again. The sheep look rather surprised, as they have a right to. They have come to be little Annie's steady company, hers and her fellow-sufferers' in the mixed-measles ward. The triangular lawn

upon which they are browsing is theirs to
gambol on when the sun shines, but cross
the walk that borders it they never can, any
more than the babies with whom they play.
Sumptuary law rules the island they are on.
Habeas corpus and the constitution stop
short of the ferry. Even Comstock's authority does not cross it: the one exception to
the rule that dolls and sheep and babies shall
not visit from ward to ward is in favor of
the rubber dolls, and the etiquette of the
island requires that they shall lay off their
woolen jackets and go calling just as the factory turned them out, without a stitch or
shred of any kind on.

As for the rest, they are assigned, babies,
nurses, sheep, rattles, and railroad-trains, to
their separate measles, scarlet-fever, and diphtheria lawns or wards, and there must be
content to stay. A sheep may be transferred
from the scarlet-fever ward with its patron
to the mixed-measles or diphtheria, when
symptoms of either of these diseases appear,
as they often do; but it cannot then go back
again, lest it carry the seeds of the new con-
tagion to its old friends.

Even the fairies are put under the ban of
suspicion by such evil associations, and, once

they have crossed the line, are not allowed to go back to corrupt the good manners of the babies with only one complaint.

Pauline Meyer, the bigger of the two girls on the mixed-measles stoop,—the other is friendless Annie,—has just enough strength to laugh when her sheep's head is pulled. She has been on the limits of one ward after another these four months, and has had everything short of typhus fever and smallpox that the island affords.

It is a marvel that there is one laugh left in her whole little shrunken body after it all; but there is, and the grin on her face reaches almost from ear to ear, as she clasps the biggest fairy in an arm very little stouter than a boy's bean-blower, and hears the lamb bleat. Why, that one smile on that ghastly face would be thought worth his fifty dollars by the children's friend, could he see it. Pauline is the child of Swedish emigrants. She and Annie will not fight over their lambs and their dolls, not for many weeks. They can't. They can't even stand up.

One of the railroad-trains, drawn by a glorious tin engine, with the name "Union" painted on the cab, is making across the stoop for the little boy with the whooping-cough in the next building. But it won't get there; it is quarantined. But it will have plenty of exercise. Little hands are itching to get hold of it in one of the cribs inside. There are thirty-six sick children on the island just now, about half of them boys, who will find plenty of use for the balls and things as soon as they get about. How those base-balls are to be kept within bounds is a hopeless mystery the doctors are puzzling over.

Even if nines are organized in every ward, as has been suggested, it is hard to see how they can be allowed to play each other, as they would want to, of course, as soon as they could toddle about. It would be something, though, a smallpox nine pitted against the scarlets or the measles, with an umpire from the mixed ward !

The old woman that lived in a shoe, being of rubber, is a privileged character, and is away on a call in the female scarlet, says the nurse. It is a good thing that she was made that way, for she is very popular. So are Mother Goose and her ten companion rubber toys. The bear and the man that strike alternately a wooden anvil with a ditto hammer are scarcely less exciting to the infantile mind; but, being of wood, they are steady boarders permanently attached each to his ward. The dominoes fell to the lot of the male scarlets. That ward has half a dozen grown men in it at present, and they have never once lost sight of the little black blocks since they first saw them.

The doctor reports that they are getting better just as fast as they can since they took to playing dominoes. If there is any hint in this to the profession at large, they are welcome to it, along with humanity.

A little girl with a rubber doll in a red-woolen jacket—a combination to make the perspiration run right off one with the humidity at 98—looks wistfully down from the second-story balcony of the smallpox pavilion, as the doctor goes past with the last sheep tucked under his arm.

But though it baa-a ever so loudly, it is not for her. It is bound for the white tent on the shore, shunned even here, where sits a solitary watcher gazing wistfully all day toward the city that has passed out of his life. Perchance it may bring to him a message from the far-away home where the birds

sang for him, and the waves and the flowers
spoke to him, and "Unclean" had not been
written against his name. Of all on the Pest
Island he alone is hopeless. He is a leper,
and his sentence is that of a living death in
a strange land.

NIGGER MARTHA'S WAKE

A WOMAN with face all seared and blotched by something that had burned through the skin sat propped up in the doorway of a Bowery restaurant at four o'clock in the morning, senseless, apparently dying. A policeman stood by, looking anxiously up the street and consulting his watch. At intervals he shook her to make sure she was not dead. The drift of the Bowery that was borne that way eddied about, intent upon what was going on. A dumpy little man edged through the crowd and peered into the woman's face.

"Phew!" he said, "it's Nigger Martha! What is gettin' into the girls on the Bowery I don't know. Remember my Maggie? She was her chum."

This to the watchman on the block. The watchman remembered. He knows everything that goes on in the Bowery. Maggie was the wayward daughter of a decent laundress, and killed herself by drinking carbolic acid less than a month before. She had wearied of the Bowery. Nigger Martha was her one friend. And now she had followed her example.

She was drunk when she did it. It is in their cups that a glimpse of the life they traded away for the street comes sometimes to these wretches, with remorse not to be borne.

It came so to Nigger Martha. Ten minutes before she had been sitting with two boon companions in the oyster saloon next door, discussing their night's catch. Elsie "Specs" was one of the two; the other was known to the street simply as Mame. Elsie wore glasses, a thing unusual enough in the Bowery to deserve recognition. From their presence Martha rose suddenly to pull a vial from her pocket. Mame saw it, and, knowing what it meant in the heavy humor that was upon Nigger Martha, she struck it from her hand with a pepper-box. It fell, but was not broken. The woman picked it up, and staggering out, swallowed its contents upon the sidewalk — that is, as much as went into her mouth.

Much went over her face, burning it. She fell shrieking.

Then came the crowd. The Bowery never sleeps. The policeman on the beat set her in the doorway and sent a hurry call for an ambulance. It came at last, and Nigger Martha was taken to the hospital.

As Mame told it, so it was recorded on the police blotter, with the addition that she was anywhere from forty to fifty years old. That was the strange part of it. It is not often that any one lasts out a generation in the Bowery. Nigger Martha did. Her beginning was way back in the palmy days of Billy McGlory and Owney Geoghegan. Her first remembered appearance was on the occasion of the mock wake they got up at Geoghegan's for Police Captain Foley when he was broken. That was in the days when dive-keepers made and broke police captains, and made no secret of it. Billy McGlory did not. Ever since, Martha was on the street.

In time she picked up Maggie Mooney, and they got to be chummy. The friendships of the Bowery by night may not be of a very exalted type, but when death breaks them it leaves nothing to the survivor. That is the reason suicides there happen in pairs. The story of Tilly Lorrison and Tricksy came from the Tenderloin not long ago. This one of Maggie Mooney and Nigger Martha was theirs over again.

In each case it was the younger, the one nearest the life that was forever past, who took the step first, in despair. The other followed. To her it was the last link with something that had long ceased to be anything but a dream, which was broken. But without the dream life was unbearable, in the Tenderloin and on the Bowery.

The newsboys were crying their night extras when Undertaker Reardon's wagon jogged across the Bowery with Nigger Martha's body in it. She had given the doctors the slip, as she had the policeman many a time. A friend of hers, an Italian in the Bend, had hired the undertaker to "do it proper," and Nigger Martha was to have a funeral.

All the Bowery came to the wake. The all-nighters from Chatham Square to Bleecker street trooped up to the top-floor flat in the Forsyth-street tenement where Nigger Martha was laid out. There they sat around, saying little and drinking much. It was not a cheery crowd.

The Bowery by night is not cheerful in

the presence of The Mystery. Its one effort
is to get away from it, to forget—the thing
it can never do. When out of its sight it
carouses boisterously, as children sing and
shout in the dark to persuade themselves that
they are not afraid. And some who hear
think it happy.

Sheeny Rose was the master of ceremonies
and kept the door. This for a purpose. In life
Nigger Martha had one enemy whom she hated
—cock-eyed Grace. Like all of her kind, Nigger Martha was superstitious. Grace's evil
eye ever brought her bad luck when she
crossed her path, and she shunned her as the
pestilence. When inadvertently she came
upon her, she turned as she passed and spat
twice over her left shoulder. And Grace, with
white malice in her wicked face, spurned her.

"I don't want," Nigger Martha had said
one night in the hearing of Sheeny Rose—
"I don't want that cock-eyed thing to look
at my body when I am dead. She'll give me
hard luck in the grave yet."

And Sheeny Rose was there to see that
cock-eyed Grace did n't come to the wake.

She did come. She labored up the long
stairs, and knocked, with no one will ever
know what purpose in her heart. If it was a

last glimmer of good, of forgiveness, it was promptly squelched. It was Sheeny Rose who opened the door.

"You can't come in here," she said curtly. "You know she hated you. She did n't want you to look at her stiff."

Cock-eyed Grace's face grew set with anger. Her curses were heard within. She threatened fight, but dropped it.

"All right," she said as she went down. "I 'll fix you, Sheeny Rose!"

It was in the exact spot where Nigger Martha had sat and died that Grace met her enemy the night after the funeral. Lizzie La Blanche, the Marine's girl, was there; Elsie Specs, Little Mame, and Jack the Dog, toughest of all the girls, who for that reason had earned the name of "Mayor of the Bowery." She brooked no rivals. They were all within reach when the two enemies met under the arc light.

Cock-eyed Grace sounded the challenge.

"Now, you little Sheeny Rose," she said, "I 'm goin' to do ye fer shuttin' of me out o' Nigger Martha's wake."

With that out came her hatpin, and she made a lunge at Sheeny Rose. The other was on her guard. Hatpin in hand, she parried the thrust and lunged back. In a moment the girls had made a ring about the two, shutting them out of sight. Within it the desperate women thrust and parried, backed and squared off, leaping like tigers when they saw an opening. Their hats had fallen off, their hair was down, and eager hate glittered in their eyes. It was a battle for life; for there is no dagger more deadly than the hatpin these women carry, chiefly as a weapon of defense in the hour of need.

They were evenly matched. Sheeny Rose made up in superior suppleness of limb for the pent-up malice of the other. Grace aimed her thrusts at her opponent's face. She tried to reach her eye. Once the sharp steel just pricked Sheeny Rose's cheek and drew blood. In the next turn Rose's hatpin passed within a quarter-inch of Grace's jugular.

But the blow nearly threw her off her feet, and she was at her enemy's mercy. With an evil oath the fiend thrust full at her face just as the policeman, who had come through the crowd unobserved, so intent was it upon the fight, knocked the steel from her hand.

At midnight two disheveled hags with faces

flattened against the bars of adjoining cells in the police station were hurling sidelong curses at each other and at the maddened doorman. Nigger Martha's wake had received its appropriate and foreordained ending.

A CHIP FROM THE MAELSTROM

"THE cop just sceert her to death, that 's
what he done. For Gawd's sake, boss,
don't let on I tole you."

The negro, stopping suddenly in his game
of craps in the Pell-street back yard, glanced
up with a look of agonized entreaty. Discovering no such fell purpose in his questioner's
face, he added quickly, reassured:

"And if he asks if you seed me a-playing
craps, say no, not on yer life, boss, will yer?"
And he resumed the game where he left off.

An hour before he had seen Maggie Lynch
die in that hallway, and it was of her he
spoke. She belonged to the tenement and to
Pell street, as he did himself. They were
part of it while they lived, with all that that
implied; when they died, to make part of it
again, reorganized and closing ranks in the
trench on Hart's Island. It is only the Celes-

tials in Pell street who escape the trench.
The others are booked for it from the day
they are pushed out from the rapids of the
Bowery into this maelstrom that sucks under
all it seizes. Thenceforward they come to
the surface only at intervals in the police
courts, each time more forlorn, but not more
hopeless, until at last they disappear and are
heard of no more.

When Maggie Lynch turned the corner no
one there knows. The street keeps no reckoning, and it does n't matter. She took her place
unchallenged, and her "character" was registered in due time. It was good. Even Pell
street has its degrees and its standard of
perfection. The standard's strong point is
contempt of the Chinese, who are hosts in
Pell street. Maggie Lynch came to be known
as homeless, without a man, though with the
prospects of motherhood approaching, yet she
"had never lived with a Chink." To Pell
street that was heroic. It would have forgiven all the rest, had there been anything
to forgive. But there was not. Whatever
else may be, cant is not among the vices of
Pell street.

And it is well. Maggie Lynch lived with
the Cuffs on the top floor of No. 21 until the

Cuffs moved.   They left an old lounge they
did n't want, and Maggie.   Maggie was sick,
and the housekeeper had no heart to put her
out.   Heart sometimes survives in the slums,
even in Pell street, long after respectability
has been hopelessly smothered.   It provided
shelter and a bed for Maggie when her only
friends deserted her.   In return she did what
she could, helping about the hall and stairs.
Queer that gratitude should be another of the
virtues the slum has no power to smother,
though dive and brothel and the scorn of the ·
good do their best, working together.

There was an old mattress that had to
be burned, and Maggie dragged it down with
an effort.   She took it out in the street, and
there set it on fire.   It burned and blazed
high in the narrow street.   The policeman
saw the sheen in the windows on the opposite
side of the way, and saw the danger of it as
he came around the corner.   Maggie did not
notice him till he was right behind her.   She
gave a great start when he spoke to her.

"I 've a good mind to lock you up for this,"
he said as he stamped out the fire.   "Don't
you know it 's against the law ?"

The negro heard it and saw Maggie stagger
toward the door, with her hand pressed upon

her heart, as the policeman went away down the street. On the threshold she stopped, panting.

"My Gawd, that cop frightened me!" she said, and sat down on the door-step.

A tenant who came out saw that she was ill, and helped her into the hall. She gasped once or twice, and then lay back, dead.

Word went around to the Elizabeth-street station, and was sent on from there with an order for the dead-wagon. Maggie's turn had come for the ride up the Sound. She was as good as checked off for the Potter's Field, but Pell street made an effort and came up almost to Maggie's standard.

Even while the dead-wagon was rattling down the Bowery, one of the tenants ran all the way to Henry street, where he had heard that Maggie's father lived, and brought him to the police station. The old man wiped his eyes as he gazed upon his child, dead in her sins.

"She had a good home," he said to Captain Young. "But she did n't know it, and she would n't stay. Send her home, and I will bury her with her mother."

The Potter's Field was cheated out of a victim, and by Pell street. But the maelstrom grinds on and on.

POLICEMAN MULLER had run against a
boisterous crowd surrounding a drunken
woman at Prince street and the Bowery.
When he joined the crowd it scattered, but
got together again before it had run half a
block, and slunk after him and his prisoner
to the Mulberry-street station. There Sergeant Woodruff learned by questioning the
woman that she was Mary Donovan and had
come down from Westchester to have a holiday. She had had it without a doubt. The
sergeant ordered her to be locked up for
safe-keeping, when, unexpectedly, objection
was made.

A small lot of the crowd had picked up
courage to come into the station to see what
became of the prisoner. From out of this, one

spoke up: "Don't lock that woman up; she is my wife."

"Eh," said the sergeant, "and who are you?"

The man said he was George Reilly and a salesman. The prisoner had given her name as Mary Donovan and said she was single. The sergeant drew Mr. Reilly's attention to the street door, which was there for his accommodation, but he did not take the hint. He became so abusive that he, too, was locked up, still protesting that the woman was his wife.

She had gone on her way to Elizabeth street, where there is a matron, to be locked up there; and the objections of Mr. Reilly having been silenced at last, peace was descending once more upon the station-house, when the door was opened, and a man with a swagger entered.

"Got that woman locked up here?" he demanded.

"What woman?" asked the sergeant, looking up.

"Her what Muller took in."

"Well," said the sergeant, looking over the desk, "what of her?"

"I want her out; she is my wife. She—"

The sergeant rang his bell. "Here, lock this man up with that woman's other husband," he said, pointing to the stranger.

The fellow ran out just in time, as the doorman made a grab for him. The sergeant drew a tired breath and picked up the ruler to make a red line in his blotter. There was a brisk step, a rap, and a young fellow stood in the open door.

"Say, serg," he began.

The sergeant reached with his left hand for the inkstand, while his right clutched the ruler. He never took his eyes off the stranger.

"Say," wheedled he, glancing around and seeing no trap, "serg, I say: that woman w'at 's locked up, she 's—"

"She 's what?" asked the sergeant, getting the range as well as he could.

"My wife," said the fellow.

There was a bang, the slamming of a door, and the room was empty. The doorman came running in, looked out, and up and down the street. But nothing was to be seen. There is no record of what became of the third husband of Mary Donovan.

The first slept serenely in the jail. The woman herself, when she saw the iron bars in the Elizabeth-street station, fell into hysterics and was taken to the Hudson Street Hospital.

Reilly was arraigned in the Tombs Police Court in the morning. He paid his fine and left, protesting that he was her only husband.

He had not been gone ten minutes when Claimant No. 4 entered.

" Was Sarah Joyce brought here ? " he asked Clerk Betts.

The clerk could n't find the name.

" Look for Mary Donovan," said No. 4.

" Who are you ? " asked the clerk.

" I am Sarah's husband," was the answer.

Clerk Betts smiled, and told the man the story of the other three.

" Well, I am blamed," he said.

THE CAT TOOK THE KOSHER MEAT

THE tenement No. 76 Madison street had been for some time scandalized by the hoidenish ways of Rose Baruch, the little cloakmaker on the top floor. Rose was seventeen, and boarded with her mother in the Pincus family. But for her harum-scarum ways she might, in the opinion of the tenement, be a nice girl and some day a good wife; but these were unbearable.

For the tenement is a great working hive in which nothing has value unless exchangeable for gold. Rose's animal spirits, which long hours and low wages had no power to curb, were exchangeable only for wrath in the tenement. Her noisy feet on the stairs when she came home woke up all the tenants, and made them swear at the loss of the precious moments of sleep which were their reserve capital. Rose was so Americanized, they said impatiently among themselves, that nothing could be done with her.

Perhaps they were mistaken. Perhaps Rose's stout refusal to be subdued even by the tenement was their hope, as it was her capital. Perhaps her spiteful tread upon the stairs heralded the coming protest of the free-born American against slavery, industrial or otherwise, in which their day of deliverance was dawning. It may be so. They did n't see it. How should they? They were not Americanized; not yet.

However that might be, Rose came to the end that was to be expected. The judgment of the tenement was, for the time, borne out by experience. This was the way of it:

Rose's mother had bought several pounds of kosher meat and put it into the ice-box— that is to say, on the window-sill of their fifth-floor flat. Other ice-box these East-Side sweaters' tenements have none. And it does well enough in cold weather, unless the cat gets around, or, as it happened in this case, it slides off and falls down. Rose's breakfast and dinner disappeared down the air-shaft, seventy feet or more, at 10 : 30 P. M.

There was a family consultation as to what

should be done.   It was late, and everybody
was in bed, but Rose declared herself equal
to the rousing of the tenants in the first
floor rear, through whose window she could
climb into the shaft for the meat.   She had
done it before for a nickel.   Enough said.
An expedition set out at once from the top
floor to recover the meat.   Mrs. Baruch,
Rose, and Jake, the boarder, went in a body.

Arrived before the Knauff family's flat on
the ground floor, they opened proceedings by
a vigorous attack on the door.   The Knauffs
woke up in a fright, believing that the house
was full of burglars.   They were stirring to
barricade the door, when they recognized
Rose's voice and were calmed.   Let in, the
expedition explained matters, and was grudg-
ingly allowed to take a look out of the window
in the air-shaft.   Yes! there was the meat, as
yet safe from rats.   The thing was to get it.

The boarder tried first, but crawled back
frightened.   He could n't reach it.   Rose
jerked him impatiently away.

"Leg go!" she said.   "I can do it.   I was
there wunst.   You 're no good."

And she bent over the window-sill, reaching
down until her toes barely touched the floor,
when all of a sudden, before they could grab

her skirts, over she went, heels over head, down the shaft, and disappeared.

The shrieks of the Knauffs, of Mrs. Baruch, and of Jake, the boarder, were echoed from below. Rose's voice rose in pain and in bitter lamentation from the bottom of the shaft. She had fallen fully fifteen feet, and in the fall had hurt her back badly, if, indeed, she had not injured herself beyond repair. Her cries suggested nothing less. They filled the tenement, rising to every floor and appealing at every bedroom window.

In a minute the whole building was astir from cellar to roof. A dozen heads were thrust out of every window, and answering wails carried messages of helpless sympathy to the once so unpopular Rose. Upon this concert of sorrow the police broke in with anxious inquiry as to what was the matter.

When they found out, a second relief expedition was organized. It reached Rose through the basement coal-bin, and she was carried out and sent to the Gouverneur Hospital. There she lies, unable to move, and the tenement wonders what is amiss that it has lost its old spirits. It has not even anything left to swear at.

The cat took the kosher meat.

FIRE IN THE BARRACKS

THE rush and roar, the blaze and the wild panic, of a great fire filled Twenty-third street. Helmeted men stormed and swore; horses tramped and reared; crying women, hurrying hither and thither, stumbled over squirming hose on street and sidewalk.

The throbbing of a dozen pumping-engines merged all other sounds in its frantic appeal for haste. In the midst of it all, seven red-shirted men knelt beside a heap of trunks, hastily thrown up as if for a breastwork, and prayed fervently with bared heads.

Firemen and policemen stumbled up against them with angry words, stopped, stared, and passed silently by. The fleeing crowd halted and fell back. The rush and the roar swirled to the right and to the left, leaving the little band as if in an eddy, untouched and serene, with the glow of the fire upon it and the stars paling overhead.

The seven were the Swedish Salvation Army. Their barracks were burning up in a blast of fire so sudden and so fierce that scant time was left to save life and goods.

From the tenements next door men and women dragged bundles and feather-beds, choking stairs and halls, and shrieking madly to be let out. The police struggled angrily with the torrent. The lodgers in the Holly-Tree Inn, who had nothing to save, ran for their lives.

In the station-house behind the barracks they were hastily clearing the prison. The last man had hardly passed out of his cell when, with a deafening crash, the toppling wall fell upon and smashed the roof of the jail.

Fire-bells rang in every street as engines rushed from north and south. A general alarm had called out the reserves. Every hydrant for blocks around was tapped. Engine crews climbed upon the track of the elevated road, picketed the surrounding tenements, and stood their ground on top of the police station.

Up there two crews labored with a Siamese joint hose throwing a stream as big as a man's thigh. It got away from them, and for a while there was panic and a struggle up on the heights as well as in the street. The throbbing hose bounded over the roof, thrashing right and left, and flinging about the men who endeavored to pin it down like half-drowned kittens. It struck the coping, knocked it off, and the resistless stream washed brick and stone down into the yard as upon the wave of a mighty flood.

Amid the fright and uproar the seven alone were calm. The sun rose upon their little band perched upon the pile of trunks, victorious and defiant. It shone upon Old Glory and the Salvation Army's flag floating from their improvised fort, and upon an ample lake, sprung up within an hour where yesterday there was a vacant sunken lot. The fire was out, the firemen going home.

The lodgers in the Holly-Tree Inn, of whom there is one for every day in the year, looked upon the sudden expanse of water, shivered, and went in. The tenants returned to their homes. The fright was over with the darkness.

A WAR ON THE GOATS

W AR has been declared in Hell's Kitchen.
An indignant public opinion demands
to have "something done ag'in' them goats,"
and there is alarm at the river end of the
street. A public opinion in Hell's Kitchen
that demands anything besides schooners of
mixed ale is a sign. Surer than a college
settlement and a sociological canvass, it fore-
tells the end of the slum. Sebastopol, the
rocky fastness of the gang that gave the place
its bad name, was razed only the other day,
and now the police have been set on the goats.
Cause enough for alarm.

A reconnaissance in force by the enemy
showed some foundation for the claim that
the goats owned the block. Thirteen were
found foraging in the gutters, standing upon
trucks, or calmly dozing in doorways. They

9   129

evinced no particularly hostile disposition, but a marked desire to know the business of every chance caller in the block. This caused a passing unpleasantness between one big white goat and the janitress of the tenement on the corner. Being crowded up against the wall by the animal, bent on exploring her pockets, she beat it off with her scrubbing-pail and mop. The goat, thus dismissed, joined a horse at the curb in apparently innocent meditation, but with one leering eye fixed back over its shoulder upon the housekeeper setting out an ash-barrel.

Her back was barely turned when it was in the barrel, with head and fore feet exploring its depths. The door of the tenement opened upon the housekeeper trundling another barrel just as the first one fell and rolled across the sidewalk, with the goat capering about. Then was the air filled with bad language and a broomstick and a goat for a moment, and the woman was left shouting her wrongs.

"What de divil good is dem goats anyhow?" she said, panting. "There's no housekeeper in de United Shtates can watch de ash-cans wid dem divil's imps around. They near killed an Eyetalian child the other day, and

two of them got basted in de neck when de
goats follied dem and did n't get nothing.
That big white one o' Tim's, he 's the worst
in de lot, and he 's got only one horn, too."

This wicked and unsymmetrical animal
is denounced for its malice throughout the
block by even the defenders of the goats.
Singularly enough, he cannot be located, and
neither can Tim. If the scouting-party has
better luck and can seize this wretched beast,
half the campaign may be over. It will be
accepted as a sacrifice by one side, and the
other is willing to give it up.

Mrs. Shallock lives in a crazy old frame
house, over a saloon. Her kitchen is ap-
proached by a sort of hen-ladder, a foot wide,
which terminates in a balcony, the whole of
which was occupied by a big gray goat. There
was not room for the police inquisitor and
the goat too, and the former had to wait till
the animal had come off his perch. Mrs.
Shallock is a widow. A load of anxiety and
concern overspread her motherly countenance
when she heard of the trouble.

"Are they after dem goats again?" she
said. "Sarah! Leho! come right here, an'
don't you go in the street again. Excuse me,
sor! but it 's all because one of dem knocked

down an old woman that used to give it a
paper every day. She is the mother of the
blind newsboy around on the avenue, an' she
used to feed an old paper to him every night.
So he follied her. That night she did n't have
any, an' when he stuck his nose in her basket
an' did n't find any, he knocked her down,
an' she bruk her arm."

Whether it was the one-horned goat that
thus insisted upon his sporting extra does not
appear. Probably it was.

"There 's neighbors lives there has got 'em
on floors," Mrs. Shallock kept on. "I 'm
paying taxes here, an' I think it 's my privi-
lege to have one little goat."

"I just wish they 'd take 'em," broke in the
widow's buxom daughter, who had appeared
in the doorway, combing her hair. "They
goes up in the hall and knocks on the door
with their horns all night. There 's sixteen
dozen of them on the stoop, if there 's one.
What good are they? Let 's sell 'em to the
butcher, mama; he 'll buy 'em for mutton,
the way he did Bill Buckley's. You know
right well he did."

"They ain't much good, that 's a fact,"
mused the widow. "But yere 's Leho; she 's
follying me around just like a child. She is

a regular pet, is Leho. We got her from Mr.
Lee, who is dead, and we called her after him,
Leho [Leo]. Take Sarah; but Leho, little
Leho, let 's keep."

Leho stuck her head in through the front
door and belied her name. If the widow keeps
her, another campaign will shortly have to be
begun in Forty-sixth street. There will be
more goats where Leho is.

Mr. Cleary lives in a rear tenement and
has only one goat. It belongs, he says, to
his little boy, and is no good except to amuse
him. Minnie is her name, and she once had
a mate. When it was sold, the boy cried so
much that he was sick for two weeks. Mr.
Cleary could n't think of parting with Minnie.

Neither will Mr. Lennon, in the next yard,
give up his. He owns the stable, he says, and
axes no odds of anybody. His goat is some
good anyhow, for it gives milk for his tea.
Says his wife, " Many is the dime it has saved
us." There are two goats in Mr. Lennon's
yard, one perched on top of a shed surveying
the yard, the other engaged in chewing at a
buck-saw that hangs on the fence.

Mrs. Buckley does not know how many
goats she has. A glance at the bigger of the
two that are stabled at the entrance to the

tenement explains her doubts, which are tem-
porary.   Mrs. Buckley says that her husband
"generally sells them away," meaning the
kids, presumably to the butcher for mutton.

"Hey, Jenny!" she says, stroking the big
one at the door.   Jenny eyes the visitor calmly,
and chews an old newspaper.   She has two
horns.

"She ain't as bad as they lets on," says
Mrs. Buckley.

The scouting party reports the new public
opinion of the Kitchen to be of healthy but
alien growth, as yet without roots in the soil
strong enough to stand the shock of a general raid on the goats.   They recommend as
a present concession the seizure of the one-
horned Billy that seems to have no friends
on the block, if indeed he belongs there, and
an ambush is being laid accordingly.

ROVER'S LAST FIGHT

THE little village of Valley Stream nestles peacefully among the woods and meadows of Long Island. The days and the years roll by uneventfully within its quiet precincts. Nothing more exciting than the arrival of a party of fishermen from the city, on a vain hunt for perch in the ponds that lie hidden among its groves and feed the Brooklyn water-works, troubles the every-day routine of the village. Two great railroad wrecks are remembered thereabouts, but these are already ancient history. Only the oldest inhabitants know of the earlier one. There has n't been as much as a sudden death in the town since, and the constable and chief of police—probably one and the same person—have n't turned an honest or dishonest penny in the whole course of their official existence. All of which is as it ought to be.

But at last something occurred that ought not to have been. The village was aroused at daybreak by the intelligence that a robbery had been committed overnight, and a murder. The house of Gabriel Dodge, a well-to-do farmer, had been sacked by thieves, who left in their trail the farmer's murdered dog. Rover was a collie, large for his kind, and quite as noisy as the rest of them. He had been left as an outside guard, according to Farmer Dodge's awkward practice. Inside, he might have been of use by alarming the folks when the thieves tried to get in. But they had only to fear his bark; his bite was harmless.

The whole of Valley Stream gathered at Farmer Dodge's house to watch, awe-struck, the mysterious movements of the police force as it went tiptoeing about, peeping into corners, secretly examining tracks in the mud, and squinting suspiciously at the brogans of the bystanders. When it had all been gone through, this record of facts bearing on the case was made:

Rover was dead.

He had apparently been smothered.

With the hand, not a rope.

There was a ladder set up against the window of the spare bedroom.

That it had not been there before was evidence that the thieves had set it up.

The window was open, and they had gone in.

Several watches, some good clothes, sundry articles of jewelry, all worth some six or seven hundred dollars, were missing and could not be found.

In conclusion, the constable put on record his belief that the thieves who had smothered the dog and set up the ladder had taken the property.

The solid citizens of the village sat upon the verdict in the store, solemnly considered it, and agreed that it was so. This point settled, there was left only the other: Who were the thieves? The solid citizens by a unanimous decision concluded that Inspector Byrnes was the man to tell them.

So they came over to New York and laid the matter before him, with a mental diagram of the village, the house, the dog, and the ladder at the window. There was just the suspicion of a twinkle in the corner of the inspector's eye as he listened gravely and then said:

"It was the spare bedroom, was n't it?"

"The spare bedroom," said the committee, in one breath.

"The only one in the house?" queried the inspector, further.

"The only one," responded the echo.

"H'm!" pondered the inspector. "You keep hands on your farm, Mr. Dodge?"

Mr. Dodge did.

"Sleep in the house?"

"Yes."

"Discharged any one lately?"

The committee rose as one man, and, staring at each other with bulging eyes, said "Jake!" all at once.

"Jakey, b' gosh!" repeated the constable to himself, kicking his own shins softly as he tugged at his beard. "Jake, by thunder!"

Jake was a boy of eighteen, who had been employed by the farmer to do chores. He was shiftless, and a week or two before had been sent away in disgrace. He had gone no one knew whither.

The committee told the inspector all about Jake, gave him a minute description of him,—of his ways, his gait, and his clothes,—and went home feeling that they had been wondrous smart in putting so sharp a man on the track

he would never have thought of if they had n't
mentioned Jake's name. All he had to do
now was to follow it to the end, and let them
know when he had reached it. And as these
good men had prophesied, even so it came to
pass.

Detectives of the inspector's staff were put
on the trail. They followed it from the Long
Island pastures across the East River to the
Bowery, and there into one of the cheap lodging-houses where thieves are turned out ready-
made while you wait. There they found Jake.

They did n't hail him at once, or clap him
into irons, as the constable from Valley Stream
would have done. They let him alone and
watched awhile to see what he was doing.
And the thing that they found him doing was
just what they expected : he was herding with
thieves. When they had thoroughly fastened
this companionship upon the lad, they arrested
the band. They were three.

They had not been locked up many hours
at Headquarters before the inspector sent for
Jake. He told him he knew all about his dis-
missal by Farmer Dodge, and asked him what
he had done to the old man. Jake blurted out
hotly, " Nothin'," and betrayed such feeling
that his questioner soon made him admit that

he was "sore on the boss." From that to telling the whole story of the robbery was only a little way, easy to travel in such company as Jake was in then. He told how he had come to New York, angry enough to do anything, and had "struck" the Bowery. Struck, too, his two friends, not the only two of that kind who loiter about that thoroughfare.

To them he told his story while waiting in the "hotel" for something to turn up, and they showed him a way to get square with the old man for what he had done to him. The farmer had money and property he would hate to lose. Jake knew the lay of the land, and could steer them straight; they would take care of the rest. "See!" said they.

Jake saw, and the sight tempted him. But in his mind's eye he saw also Rover and heard him bark. How could he be managed?

"He will come to me if I call him," pondered Jake, while his two companions sat watching his face, "but you may have to kill him. Poor Rover!"

"You call the dog and leave him to me," said the oldest thief, and shut his teeth hard. And so it was arranged.

That night the three went out on the last train, and hid in the woods down by the gate-

keeper's house at the pond, until the last light
had gone out in the village and it was fast
asleep.   Then they crept up by a back way to
Farmer Dodge's house.   As expected, Rover
came bounding out at their approach, barking
furiously.   It was Jake's turn then.

"Rover," he called softly, and whistled.
The dog stopped barking and came on, wag-
ging his tail, but still growling ominously as
he got scent of the strange men.

"Rover, poor Rover," said Jake, stroking his
shaggy fur and feeling like the guilty wretch
he was; for just then the hand of Pfeiffer, the
thief, grabbed the throat of the faithful beast
in a grip as of an iron vise, and he had barked
his last bark.   Struggle as he might, he could
not free himself or breathe, while Jake, the
treacherous Jake, held his legs.   And so he
died, fighting for his master and his home.

In the morning the ladder at the open window and poor Rover dead in the yard told of
the drama of the night.

The committee of farmers came over and
took Jake home, after congratulating Inspector Byrnes on having so intelligently followed
their directions in hunting down the thieves.
The inspector shook hands with them and
smiled.

WHEN THE LETTER CAME

"TO-MORROW it will come," Godfrey Krueger had said that night to his landlord. "To-morrow it will surely come, and then I shall have money. Soon I shall be rich, richer than you can think."

And the landlord of the Forsyth-street tenement, who in his heart liked the gray-haired inventor, but who had rooms to let, grumbled something about a to-morrow that never came.

"Oh, but it will come," said Krueger, turning on the stairs and shading the lamp with his hand, the better to see his landlord's good-natured face; "you know the application has been advanced. It is bound to be granted, and to-night I shall finish my ship."

Now, as he sat alone in his room at his work, fitting, shaping, and whittling with restless hands, he had to admit to himself that it was

142

time it came. Two whole days he had lived
on a crust, and he was starving. He had
worked and waited thirteen hard years for the
success that had more than once been almost
within his grasp, only to elude it again. It
had never seemed nearer and surer than now,
and there was need of it. He had come to the
jumping-off place. All his money was gone,
to the last cent, and his application for a pension hung fire in Washington unaccountably.
It had been advanced to the last stage, and
word that it had been granted might be received any day. But the days slipped by and
no word came. For two days he had lived on
faith and a crust, but they were giving out
together. If only—

Well, when it did come, what with his back
pay for all those years, he would have the
means to build his ship, and hunger and want
would be forgotten. He should have enough.
And the world would know that Godfrey
Krueger was not an idle crank.

"In six months I shall cross the ocean to
Europe in twenty hours in my air-ship," he had
said in showing the landlord his models, " with
as many as want to go. Then I shall become
a millionaire and shall make you one, too."
And the landlord had heaved a sigh at the

thought of his twenty-seven dollars, and doubtingly wished it might be so.

Weak and famished, Krueger bent to his all but finished task. Before morning he should know that it would work as he had planned. There remained only to fit the last parts together. The idea of building an air-ship had come to him while he lay dying with scurvy, as they thought, in a Confederate prison, and he had never abandoned it. He had been a teacher and a student, and was a trained mathematician. There could be no flaw in his calculations. He had worked them out again and again. The energy developed by his plan was great enough to float a ship capable of carrying almost any burden, and of directing it against the strongest head winds. Now, upon the threshold of success, he was awaiting merely the long-delayed pension to carry his dream into life. To-morrow would bring it, and with it an end to all his waiting and suffering.

One after another the lights went out in the tenement. Only the one in the inventor's room burned steadily through the night. The policeman on the beat noticed the lighted window, and made a mental note of the fact that some one was sick. Once during the early hours he stopped short to listen. Upon the morning breeze was borne a muffled sound, as of a distant explosion. But all was quiet again, and he went on, thinking that his senses had deceived him. The dawn came in the eastern sky, and with it the stir that attends the awakening of another day. The lamp burned steadily yet behind the dim window-pane.

The milkmen came, and the push-cart criers. The policeman was relieved, and another took his place. Lastly came the mailcarrier with a large official envelop marked, "Pension Bureau, Washington." He shouted up the stairway:

"Krueger! Letter!"

The landlord came to the door and was glad. So it had come, had it?

"Run, Emma," he said to his little daughter, "run and tell Mr. Godfrey his letter has come."

The child skipped up the steps gleefully. She knocked at the inventor's door, but no answer came. It was not locked, and she pushed it open. The little lamp smoked yet on the table. The room was strewn with broken models and torn papers that littered the floor. Something there frightened the child. She held to the banisters and called faintly:

"Papa! Oh, papa!"

10

They went in together on tiptoe without knowing why, the postman with the big official letter in his hand. The morrow had kept its promise. Of hunger and want there was an end. On the bed, stretched at full length, with his Grand Army hat flung beside him, lay the inventor, dead. A little round hole in the temple, from which a few drops of blood had flowed, told what remained of his story. In the night disillusion had come, with failure.

THE KID

HE was an every-day tough, bull-necked, square-jawed, red of face, and with his hair cropped short in the fashion that rules at Sing Sing and is admired of Battle Row. Any one could have told it at a glance. The bruised and wrathful face of the policeman who brought him to Mulberry street, to be "stood up" before the detectives in the hope that there might be something against him to aggravate the offense of beating an officer with his own club, bore witness to it. It told a familiar story. The prisoner's gang had started a fight in the street, probably with a scheme of ultimate robbery in view, and the police had come upon it unexpectedly. The rest had got away with an assortment of promiscuous bruises. The "Kid" stood his

147

ground, and went down with two "cops" on top of him after a valiant battle, in which he had performed the feat that entitled him to honorable mention henceforth in the felonious annals of the gang. There was no surrender in his sullen look as he stood before the desk, his hard face disfigured further by a streak of half-dried blood, reminiscent of the night's encounter. The fight had gone against him —that was all right. There was a time for getting square. Till then he was man enough to take his medicine, let them do their worst.

It was there, plain as could be, in his set jaws and dogged bearing as he came out, numbered now and indexed in the rogues' gallery, and started for the police court between two officers. It chanced that I was going the same way, and joined company. Besides, I have certain theories concerning toughs which my friend the sergeant says are rot, and I was not averse to testing them on the Kid.

But the Kid was a bad subject. He replied to my friendly advances with a muttered curse, or not at all, and upset all my notions in the most reckless way. Conversation had ceased before we were half-way across to Broadway. He "wanted no guff," and I left

him to his meditations respecting his defense-
less state. At Broadway there was a jam of
trucks, and we stopped at the corner to wait
for an opening.

It all happened so quickly that only a con-
fused picture of it is in my mind till this day.
A sudden start, a leap, and a warning cry, and
the Kid had wrenched himself loose. He was
free. I was dimly conscious of a rush of blue
and brass; and then I saw—the whole street
saw—a child, a toddling baby, in the middle
of the railroad-track, right in front of the coming car. It reached out its tiny hand toward
the madly clanging bell and crowed. A scream
rose wild and piercing above the tumult; men
struggled with a frantic woman on the curb,
and turned their heads away—

And then there stood the Kid, with the
child in his arms, unhurt. I see him now, as
he set it down gently as any woman, trying,
with lingering touch, to unclasp the grip of
the baby hand upon his rough finger. I see
the hard look coming back into his face as the
policeman, red and out of breath, twisted the
nipper on his wrist, with a half-uncertain
aside to me: "Them toughs there ain't no
depending on nohow." Sullen, defiant, plan-
ning vengeance, I see him led away to jail.

Ruffian and thief! The police blotter said so.

But, even so, the Kid had proved that my theories about toughs were not rot. Who knows but that, like sergeants, the blotter may be sometimes mistaken?

LOST CHILDREN

I AM not thinking now of theological dogmas or moral distinctions. I am considering the matter from the plain every-day standpoint of the police office. It is not my fault that the one thing that is lost more persistently than any other in a large city is the very thing you would imagine to be safest of all in the keeping of its owner. Nor do I pretend to explain it. It is simply one of the contradictions of metropolitan life. In twenty years' acquaintance with the police office, I have seen money, diamonds, coffins, horses, and tubs of butter brought there and passed into the keeping of the property clerk as lost or strayed. I remember a whole front stoop, brownstone, with steps and iron railing all complete, being put up at auction, unclaimed. But these were mere representatives of a class which as a whole kept its place and the peace. The children did neither. One might have been tempted to apply the old inquiry about the pins to them but for another contradictory circumstance: rather more of them are found than lost.

The Society for the Prevention of Cruelty to Children keeps the account of the surplus. It has now on its books half a score Jane Does and twice as many Richard Roes, of whom nothing more will ever be known than that they were found, which is on the whole, perhaps, best—for them certainly. The others, the lost, drift from the tenements and back, a host of thousands year by year. The two I am thinking of were of these, typical of the maelstrom.

Yette Lubinsky was three years old when she was lost from her Essex-street home, in that neighborhood where once the police commissioners thought seriously of having the children tagged with name and street number, to save trotting them back and forth between police station and Headquarters. She had gone from the tenement to the corner where her father kept a stand, to beg a penny, and nothing more was known of her. Weeks after, a neighbor identified one of her little

frocks as the match of one worn by a child
she had seen dragged off by a rough-looking
man. But though Max Lubinsky, the peddler,
and Yette's mother camped on the steps of
Police Headquarters early and late, anxiously
questioning every one who went in and out
about their lost child, no other word was
heard of her. By and by it came to be an
old story, and the two were looked upon as
among the fixtures of the place. Mulberry
street has other such.

They were poor and friendless in a strange
land, the very language of which was jargon
to them, as theirs was to us, timid in the
crush, and they were shouldered out. It was
not inhumanity; at least, it was not meant to
be. It was the way of the city, with every
one for himself; and they accepted it, uncom-
plaining. So they kept their vigil on the
stone steps, in storm and fair weather, every
night, taking turns to watch all who passed.
When it was a policeman with a little child,
as it was many times between sunset and sun-
rise, the one on the watch would start up the
minute they turned the corner, and run to
meet them, eagerly scanning the little face,
only to return, disappointed but not cast
down, to the step upon which the other slept,

head upon knees, waiting the summons to wake and watch.

Their mute sorrow appealed to me, then doing night duty in the newspaper office across the way, and I tried to help them in their search for the lost Yette. They accepted my help gratefully, trustfully, but without loud demonstration. Together we searched the police records, the hospitals, the morgue, and the long register of the river's dead. She was not there. Having made sure of this, we turned to the children's asylums. We had a description of Yette sent to each and every one, with the minutest particulars concerning her and her disappearance, but no word came back in response. A year passed, and we were compelled at last to give over the search. It seemed as if every means of finding out what had become of the child had been exhausted, and all alike had failed.

During the long search, I had occasion to go more than once to the Lubinskys' home. They lived up three flights, in one of the big barracks that give to the lower end of Essex street the appearance of a deep black cañon with cliff-dwellers living in tiers all the way up, their watch-fires showing like so many dull red eyes through the night. The hall was pitch-dark, and the whole building redolent of the slum; but in the stuffy little room where the peddler lived there was, in spite of it all, an atmosphere of home that set it sharply apart from the rest. One of these visits I will always remember. I had stumbled in, unthinking, upon their Sabbath-eve meal. The candles were lighted, and the children gathered about the table; at its head, the father, every trace of the timid, shrinking peddler of Mulberry street laid aside with the week's toil, was invoking the Sabbath blessing upon his house and all it harbored. I saw him turn, with a quiver of the lip, to a vacant seat between him and the mother; and it was then that I noticed the baby's high chair, empty, but kept ever waiting for the little wanderer. I understood; and in the strength of domestic affection that burned with unquenched faith in the dark tenement after the many months of weary failure I read the history of this strange people that in every land and in every day has conquered even the slum with the hope of home.

It was not to be put to shame here, either. Yette returned, after all, and the way of it came near being stranger than all the rest. Two long years had passed, and the memory of her and hers had long since faded out of Mulberry street, when, in the overhauling of one of the children's homes we thought we had canvassed thoroughly, the child turned up, as unaccountably as she had been lost. All that I ever learned about it was that she had been brought there, picked up by some one in the street, probably, and, after more or less inquiry that had failed to connect with the search at our end of the line, had been included in their flock on some formal commitment, and had stayed there. Not knowing her name,—she could not tell it herself, to be understood,—they had given her one of their own choosing; and thus disguised, she might have stayed there forever but for the fortunate chance that cast her up to the surface once more, and gave the clue to her identity at last. Even then her father had nearly as much trouble in proving his title to his child as he had had in looking for her, but in the end he made it good. The frock she had worn when she was lost proved the missing link. The mate of it was still carefully laid away in the tenement. So Yette returned to fill the empty chair at the Sabbath board, and the peddler's faith was justified.

My other chip from the maelstrom was a lad
half grown. He dropped into my office as
if out of the clouds, one long and busy day,
when, tired and out of sorts, I sat wishing
my papers and the world in general in Hali-
fax. I had not heard the knock, and when I
looked up, there stood my boy, a stout, square-
shouldered lad, with heavy cowhide boots and
dull, honest eyes—eyes that looked into mine
as if with a question they were about to put,
and then gave it up, gazing straight ahead,
stolid, impassive. It struck me that I had
seen that face before, and I found out immediately where. The officer of the Children's
Aid Society who had brought him explained
that Frands—that was his name—had been
in the society's care five months and over.
They had found him drifting in the streets,
and, knowing whither that drift set, had taken
him in charge and sent him to one of their
lodging-houses, where he had been since, doing
chores and plodding about in his dull way.
That was where I had met him. Now they
had decided that he should go to Florida, if
he would, but first they would like to find out
something about him. They had never been
able to, beyond the fact that he was from

Denmark. He had put his finger on the map in the reading-room, one day, and shown them where he came from: that was the extent of their information on that point. So they had sent him to me to talk to him in his own tongue and see what I could make of him.

I addressed him in the politest Danish I was master of, and for an instant I saw the listening, questioning look return; but it vanished almost at once, and he answered in monosyllables, if at all. Much of what I said passed him entirely by. He did not seem to understand. By slow stages I got out of him that his father was a farm-laborer; that he had come over to look for his cousin, who worked in Passaic, New Jersey, and had found him,— Heaven knows how !—but had lost him again. Then he had drifted to New York, where the society's officers had come upon him. He nodded when told that he was to be sent far away to the country, much as if I had spoken of some one he had never heard of. We had arrived at this point when I asked him the name of his native town.

The word he spoke came upon me with all the force of a sudden blow. I had played in the old village as a boy ; all my childhood was bound up in its memories. For many years

now I had not heard its name—not since boyhood days spoken as he spoke it. Perhaps it
was because I was tired: the office faded
away, desk, Headquarters across the street,
boy, officer, business, and all. In their place
were the brown heath I loved, the distant
hills, the winding wagon-track, the peat-
stacks, and the solitary sheep browsing on
the barrows. Forgotten the thirty years, the
seas that rolled between, the teeming city! I
was at home again, a child. And there he
stood, the boy, with it all in his dull, absent
look. I read it now as plain as the day.

"Hua er et no? Ka do ett fostó hua a
sejer?"

- It plumped out of me in the broad Jutland
dialect I had neither heard nor spoken in half
a lifetime, and so astonished me that I nearly
fell off my chair. Sheep, peat-stacks, cairn,
and hills all vanished together, and in place
of the sweet heather there was the table with
the tiresome papers. I reached out yearningly
after the heath; I had not seen it for such a
long time,—how long it did seem!—and—but
in the same breath it was all there again in
the smile that lighted up Frands's broad
face like a glint of sunlight from a leaden
sky.

"Joesses, jou," he laughed, "no ka a da saa grou godt."[1]

It was the first honest Danish word he had heard since he came to this bewildering land. I read it in his face, no longer heavy or dull; saw it in the way he followed my speech—spelling the words, as it were, with his own lips, to lose no syllable; caught it in his glad smile as he went on telling me about his journey, his home, and his homesickness for the heath, with a breathless kind of haste, as if, now that at last he had a chance, he were afraid it was all a dream, and that he would presently wake up and find it gone. Then the officer pulled my sleeve.

He had coughed once or twice, but neither of us had heard him. Now he held out a paper he had brought, with an apologetic gesture. It was an agreement Frands was to sign, if he was going to Florida. I glanced at it. Florida? Yes, to be sure; oh, yes, Florida. I spoke to the officer, and it was in the Jutland dialect. I tried again, with no better luck. I saw him looking at me queerly,

[1] My exclamation on finding myself so suddenly translated back to Denmark was an impatient "Why, don't you understand me?" His answer was, "Lord, yes, now I do, indeed."

as if he thought it was not quite right with me, either, and then I recovered myself, and got back to the office and to America; but it was an effort. One does not skip across thirty years and two oceans, at my age, so easily as that.

And then the dull look came back into Frands's eyes, and he nodded stolidly. Yes, he would go to Florida. The papers were made out, and off he went, after giving me a hearty hand-shake that warranted he would come out right when he became accustomed to the new country; but he took something with him which it hurt me to part with.

FRANDS is long since in Florida, growing up with the country, and little Yette is a young woman. So long ago was it that the current which sucked her under cast her up again, that there lives not in the whole street any one who can recall her loss. I tried to find one only the other day, but all the old people were dead or had moved away, and of the young, who were very anxious to help me, scarcely one was born at that time. But still the maelstrom drags down its victims; and far away lies my Danish heath under the gray October sky, hidden behind the seas.

11

THE SLIPPER-MAKER'S FAST

ISAAC JOSEPHS, slipper-maker, sat up on the fifth floor of his Allen-street tenement, in the gray of the morning, to finish the task he had set himself before Yom Kippur. Three days and three nights he had worked without sleep, almost without taking time to eat, to make ready the two dozen slippers that were to enable him to fast the fourth day and night for conscience' sake, and now they were nearly done. As he saw the end of his task near, he worked faster and faster, while the tenement slept.

Three years he had slaved for the sweater, stinted and starved himself, before he had saved enough to send for his wife and children, awaiting his summons in the city by the Black Sea. Since they came they had slaved and starved together; for wages had become stead-

162

ily less, work more grinding, and hours longer
and later. Still, of that he thought little.
They had known little else, there or here, and
they were together now. The past was dead;
the future was their own, even in the Allen-
street tenement, toiling night and day at starvation wages. To-morrow was the feast, their
first Yom Kippur since they had come together
again,—Esther, his wife, and Ruth and little
Ben,—the feast when, priest and patriarch of
his own house, he might forget his bondage
and be free. Poor little Ben! The hand that
smoothed the soft leather on the last took a
tenderer, lingering touch as he glanced toward
the stool where the child had sat watching him
work till his eyes grew small. Brave little
Ben, almost a baby yet, but so patient, so
wise, and so strong!

The deep breathing of the sleeping children
reached him from their crib. He smiled and
listened, with the half-finished slipper in his
hand. As he sat thus, a great drowsiness
came upon him. He nodded once, twice; his
hands sank into his lap, his head fell forward
upon his chest. In the silence of the morning
he slept, worn out with utter weariness.

He awoke with a guilty start to find the
first rays of the dawn struggling through his

window, and his task yet undone. With desperate energy he seized the unfinished slipper to resume his work. His unsteady hand upset the little lamp by his side, upon which his burnishing-iron was heating. The oil blazed up on the floor and ran toward the nearly finished pile of work. The cloth on the table caught fire. In a fever of terror and excitement, the slipper-maker caught it in his hands, wrung it, and tore at it to smother the flames. His hands were burned, but what of that? The slippers, the slippers! If they were burned, it was ruin. There would be no Yom Kippur, no feast of Atonement, no fast —rather, no end of it; starvation for him and his.

He beat the fire with his hands and trampled it with his feet as it burned and spread on the floor. His hair and his beard caught fire. With a despairing shriek he gave it up and fell before the precious slippers, barring the way of the flames to them with his body.

The shriek woke his wife. She sprang out of bed, snatched up a blanket, and threw it upon the fire. It went out, was smothered under the blanket. The slipper-maker sat up, panting and grateful. His Yom Kippur was saved.

The tenement awoke to hear of the fire in the morning, when all Jewtown was stirring with preparations for the feast. The slipper-maker's wife was setting the house to rights for the holiday then. Two half-naked children played about her knees, asking eager questions about it. Asked if her husband had often to work so hard, and what he made by it, she shrugged her shoulders and said : " The rent and a crust."

And yet all this labor and effort to enable him to fast one day according to the old dispensation, when all the rest of the days he fasted according to the new !

PAOLO'S AWAKENING

PAOLO sat cross-legged on his bench, stitching away for dear life. He pursed his lips and screwed up his mouth into all sorts of odd shapes with the effort, for it was an effort. He was only eight, and you would scarcely have imagined him over six, as he sat there sewing like a real little tailor; only Paolo knew but one seam, and that a hard one. Yet he held the needle and felt the edge with it in quite a grown-up way, and pulled the thread just as far as his short arm would reach. His mother sat on a stool by the window, where she could help him when he got into a snarl,—as he did once in a while, in spite of all he could do,—or when the needle had to be threaded. Then she dropped her own sewing, and, patting him on the head, said he was a good boy.

166

Paolo felt very proud and big then, that he was able to help his mother, and he worked even more carefully and faithfully than before, so that the boss should find no fault. The shouts of the boys in the block, playing duck-on-a-rock down in the street, came in through the open window, and he laughed as he heard them. He did not envy them, though he liked well enough to romp with the others. His was a sunny temper, content with what came; besides, his supper was at stake, and Paolo had a good appetite. They were in sober earnest working for dear life—Paolo and his mother.

" Pants" for the sweater in Stanton street was what they were making; little knicker-bockers for boys of Paolo's own age. " Twelve pants for ten cents," he said, counting on his fingers. The mother brought them once a week—a big bundle which she carried home on her head—to have the buttons put on, fourteen on each pair, the bottoms turned up, and a ribbon sewed fast to the back seam inside. That was called finishing. When work was brisk—and it was not always so since there had been such frequent strikes in Stanton street—they could together make the rent-money, and even more, as Paolo was learning

and getting a stronger grip on the needle
week by week.   The rent was six dollars a
month for a dingy basement room, in which
it was twilight even on the brightest days,
and a dark little cubbyhole, where it was
always midnight, and where there was just
room for a bed of old boards, no more.   In
there slept Paolo with his uncle; his mother
made her bed on the floor of the "kitchen,"
as they called it.

The three made the family.   There used to
be four; but one stormy night in winter Paolo's
father had not come home.   The uncle
came alone, and the story he told made the
poor home in the basement darker and drearier
for many a day than it had yet been.   The
two men worked together for a padrone on
the scows.   They were in the crew that went
out that day to the dumping-ground, far outside the harbor.   It was a dangerous journey
in a rough sea.   The half-frozen Italians clung
to the great heaps like so many frightened
flies, when the waves rose and tossed the
unwieldy scows about, bumping one against
the other, though they were strung out in a
long row behind the tug, quite a distance
apart.   One sea washed entirely over the last
scow and nearly upset it.   When it floated

even again, two of the crew were missing, one of them Paolo's father. They had been washed away and lost, miles from shore. No one ever saw them again.

The widow's tears flowed for her dead husband, whom she could not even see laid in a grave which the priest had blessed. The good father spoke to her of the sea as a vast God's-acre, over which the storms are forever chanting anthems in his praise to whom the secrets of its depths are revealed; but she thought of it only as the cruel destroyer that had robbed her of her husband, and her tears fell faster. Paolo cried, too: partly because his mother cried; partly, if the truth must be told, because he was not to have a ride to the cemetery in the splendid coach. Giuseppe Salvatore, in the corner house, had never ceased talking of the ride he had when his father died, the year before. Pietro and Jim went along, too, and rode all the way behind the hearse with black plumes. It was a sore subject with Paolo, for he was in school that day.

And then he and his mother dried their tears and went to work. Henceforth there was to be little else for them. The luxury of grief is not among the few luxuries which

Mott-street tenements afford.　Paolo's life, after that, was lived mainly with the pants on his hard bench in the rear tenement.　His routine of work was varied by the household duties, which he shared with his mother. There were the meals to get, few and plain as they were.　Paolo was the cook, and not infrequently, when a building was being torn down in the neighborhood, he furnished the fuel as well.　Those were his off days, when he put the needle away and foraged with the other children, dragging old beams and carrying burdens far beyond his years.

The truant officer never found his way to Paolo's tenement to discover that he could neither read nor write, and, what was more, would probably never learn.　It would have been of little use, for the public schools thereabouts were crowded, and Paolo could not have got into one of them if he had tried. The teacher from the Industrial School, which he had attended for one brief season while his father was alive, called at long intervals, and brought him once a plant, which he set out in his mother's window-garden and nursed carefully ever after.　The " garden " was contained within an old starch-box, which had its place on the window-sill since the policeman had ordered the fire-escape to be cleared. It was a kitchen-garden with vegetables, and was almost all the green there was in the landscape. From one or two other windows in the yard there peeped tufts of green; but of trees there was none in sight—nothing but the bare clothes-poles with their pulley-lines stretching from every window.

Beside the cemetery plot in the next block there was not an open spot or breathing-place, certainly not a playground, within reach of that great teeming slum that harbored more than a hundred thousand persons, young and old. Even the graveyard was shut in by a high brick wall, so that a glimpse of the greensward over the old mounds was to be caught only through the spiked iron gates, the key to which was lost, or by standing on tiptoe and craning one's neck. The dead there were of more account, though they had been forgotten these many years, than the living children who gazed so wistfully upon the little paradise through the barred gates, and were chased by the policeman when he came that way. Something like this thought was in Paolo's mind when he stood at sunset and peered in at the golden rays

falling athwart the green, but he did not
know it.   Paolo was not a philosopher, but
he loved beauty and beautiful things, and was
conscious of a great hunger which there was
nothing in his narrow world to satisfy.

Certainly not in the tenement.   It was old
and rickety and wretched, in keeping with
the slum of which it formed a part.   The
whitewash was peeling off the walls, the stairs
were patched, and the door-step long since
worn entirely away.   It was hard to be
decent in such a place, but the widow did
the best she could.   Her rooms were as neat
as the general dilapidation would permit.   On
the shelf where the old clock stood, flanked
by the best crockery, most of it cracked and
yellow with age, there was red and green
paper cut in scallops very nicely.   Garlic and
onions hung in strings over the stove, and
the red peppers that grew in the starch-box
at the window gave quite a cheerful appearance to the room.   In the corner, under a
cheap print of the Virgin Mary with the
Child, a small night-light in a blue glass was
always kept burning.   It was a kind of
illumination in honor of the Mother of God,
through which the widow's devout nature
found expression.   Paolo always looked upon

it as a very solemn show. When he said his prayers, the sweet, patient eyes in the picture seemed to watch him with a mild look that made him turn over and go to sleep with a sigh of contentment. He felt then that he had not been altogether bad, and that he was quite safe in their keeping.

Yet Paolo's life was not wholly without its bright spots. Far from it. There were the occasional trips to the dump with Uncle Pasquale's dinner, where there was always sport to be had in chasing the rats that over-ran the place, fighting for the scraps and bones the trimmers had rescued from the scows. There were so many of them, and so bold were they, that an old Italian who could no longer dig was employed to sit on a bale of rags and throw things at them, lest they carry off the whole establishment. When he hit one, the rest squealed and scampered away; but they were back again in a minute, and the old man had his hands full pretty nearly all the time. Paolo thought that his was a glorious job, as any boy might, and hoped that he would soon be old, too, and as important. And then the men at the cage— a great wire crate into which the rags from the ash-barrels were stuffed, to be plunged into the river, where the tide ran through them and carried some of the loose dirt away. That was called washing the rags. To Paolo it was the most exciting thing in the world. What if some day the crate should bring up a fish, a real fish, from the river? When he thought of it, he wished that he might be sitting forever on that string-piece, fishing with the rag-cage, particularly when he was tired of stitching and turning over, a whole long day.

Besides, there were the real holidays, when there was a marriage, a christening, or a funeral in the tenement, particularly when a baby died whose father belonged to one of the many benefit societies. A brass band was the proper thing then, and the whole block took a vacation to follow the music and the white hearse out of their ward into the next. But the chief of all the holidays came once a year, when the feast of St. Rocco—the patron saint of the village where Paolo's parents had lived — was celebrated. Then a really beautiful altar was erected at one end of the yard, with lights and pictures on it. The rear fire-escapes in the whole row were decked with sheets, and made into handsome balconies,—reserved seats, as it were,— on which the tenants sat and enjoyed it. A band in gorgeous uniforms played three whole days in the yard, and the men in their holiday clothes stepped up, bowed, and crossed themselves, and laid their gifts on the plate which St. Rocco's namesake, the saloon-keeper in the block, who had got up the celebration, had put there for them. In the evening they set off great strings of fire-crackers in the street, in the saint's honor, until the police interfered once and forbade that. Those were great days for Paolo always.

But the fun Paolo loved best of all was when he could get in a corner by himself, with no one to disturb him, and build castles and things out of some abandoned clay or mortar, or wet sand if there was nothing better. The plastic material took strange shapes of beauty under his hands. It was as if life had been somehow breathed into it by his touch, and it ordered itself as none of the other boys could make it. His fingers were tipped with genius, but he did not know it, for his work was only for the hour. He destroyed it as soon as it was made, to try for something better. What he had made never satisfied him — one of the surest proofs that he was capable of great things, had he only known it. But, as I said, he did not.

The teacher from the Industrial School came upon him one day, sitting in the corner by himself, and breathing life into the mud. She stood and watched him awhile, unseen, getting interested, almost excited, as he worked on. As for Paolo, he was solving the problem that had eluded him so long, and had eyes or thought for nothing else. As his fingers ran over the soft clay, the needle, the hard bench, the pants, even the sweater himself, vanished out of his sight, out of his life, and he thought only of the beautiful things he was fashioning to express the longing in his soul, which nothing mortal could shape. Then, suddenly, seeing and despairing, he dashed it to pieces, and came back to earth and to the tenement.

But not to the pants and the sweater. What the teacher had seen that day had set her to thinking, and her visit resulted in a great change for Paolo. She called at night and had a long talk with his mother and uncle through the medium of the priest, who interpreted when they got to a hard place. Uncle Pasquale took but little part in the conversation. He sat by and nodded

most of the time, assured by the presence
of the priest that it was all right. The widow
cried a good deal, and went more than once
to take a look at the boy, lying snugly tucked
in his bed in the inner room, quite un-
conscious of the weighty matters that were
being decided concerning him. She came
back the last time drying her eyes, and laid
both her hands in the hand of the teacher.
She nodded twice and smiled through her
tears, and the bargain was made. Paolo's
slavery was at an end.

His friend came the next day and took him
away, dressed up in his best clothes, to a
large school where there were many children,
not of his own people, and where he was received kindly. There dawned that day a new
life for Paolo, for in the afternoon trays of
modeling-clay were brought in, and the children were told to mold in it objects that were
set before them. Paolo's teacher stood by,
and nodded approvingly as his little fingers
played so deftly with the clay, his face all
lighted up with joy at this strange kind of a
school-lesson.

After that he had a new and faithful friend,
and, as he worked away, putting his whole
young soul into the tasks that filled it with

radiant hope, other friends, rich and powerful, found him out in his slum. They brought
better-paying work for his mother than sewing pants for the sweater, and Uncle Pasquale
abandoned the scows to become a porter in a
big shipping-house on the West Side. The
little family moved out of the old home into
a better tenement, though not far away.
Paolo's loyal heart clung to the neighborhood where he had played and dreamed as a
child, and he wanted it to share in his good
fortune, now that it had come. As the days
passed, the neighbors who had known him as
little Paolo came to speak of him as one who
some day would be a great artist and make
them all proud. He laughed at that, and
said that the first bust he would hew in
marble should be that of his patient, faithful
mother; and with that he gave her a little
hug, and danced out of the room, leaving her
to look after him with glistening eyes, brim-
ming over with happiness.

But Paolo's dream was to have another
awakening. The years passed and brought
their changes. In the manly youth who
came forward as his name was called in the
academy, and stood modestly at the desk to
receive his diploma, few would have recog-

nized the little ragamuffin who had dragged
bundles of fire-wood to the rookery in the
alley, and carried Uncle Pasquale's dinner-
pail to the dump. But the audience gathered to witness the commencement exercises
knew it all, and greeted him with a hearty
welcome that recalled his early struggles and
his hard-won success. It was Paolo's day of
triumph. The class honors and the medal
were his. The bust that had won both stood
in the hall crowned with laurel — an Italian
peasant woman, with sweet, gentle face, in
which there lingered the memories of the
patient eyes that had lulled the child to
sleep in the old days in the alley. His
teacher spoke to him, spoke of him, with
pride in voice and glance; spoke tenderly
of his old mother of the tenement, of his
faithful work, of the loyal manhood that
ever is the soul and badge of true genius.
As he bade him welcome to the fellowship of
artists who in him honored the best and
noblest in their own aspirations, the emotion
of the audience found voice once more. Paolo, flushed, his eyes filled with happy tears,
stumbled out, he knew not how, with the
coveted parchment in his hand.

Home to his mother! It was the one

thought in his mind as he walked toward the big bridge to cross to the city of his home — to tell her of his joy, of his success. Soon she would no longer be poor. The day of hardship was over. He could work now and earn money, much money, and the world would know and honor Paolo's mother as it had honored him. As he walked through the foggy winter day toward the river, where delayed throngs jostled one another at the bridge entrance, he thought with grateful heart of the friends who had smoothed the way for him. Ah, not for long the fog and slush! The medal carried with it a traveling stipend, and soon the sunlight of his native land for him and her. He should hear the surf wash on the shingly beach and in the deep grottoes of which she had sung to him when a child. Had he not promised her this? And had they not many a time laughed for very joy at the prospect, the two together?

He picked his way up the crowded stairs, carefully guarding the precious roll. The crush was even greater than usual. There had been delay — something wrong with the cable; but a train was just waiting, and he hurried on board with the rest, little heeding what became of him so long as the diploma was safe. The train rolled out on the bridge, with Paolo wedged in the crowd on the platform of the last car, holding the paper high over his head, where it was sheltered safe from the fog and the rain and the crush.

Another train backed up, received its load of cross humanity, and vanished in the mist. The damp gray curtain had barely closed behind it, and the impatient throng was fretting at a further delay, when consternation spread in the bridge-house. Word had come up from the track that something had happened. Trains were stalled all along the route. While the dread and uncertainty grew, a messenger ran up, out of breath. There had been a collision. The last train had run into the one preceding it, in the fog. One was killed, others were injured. Doctors and ambulances were wanted.

They came with the police, and by and by the partly wrecked train was hauled up to the platform. When the wounded had been taken to the hospital, they bore from the train the body of a youth, clutching yet in his hand a torn, blood-stained paper, tied about with a purple ribbon. It was Paolo. The awakening had come. Brighter skies than those of sunny Italy had dawned upon him in the gloom and terror of the great crash. Paolo was at home, waiting for his mother.

THE
LITTLE DOLLAR'S CHRISTMAS JOURNEY

"IT is too bad," said Mrs. Lee, and she put down the magazine in which she had been reading of the poor children in the tenements of the great city that know little of Christmas joys; "no Christmas tree! One of them shall have one, at any rate. I think this will buy it, and it is so handy to send. Nobody would know that there was money in the letter." And she inclosed a coupon in a letter to a professor, a friend in the city, who, she knew, would have no trouble in finding the child, and had it mailed at once. Mrs. Lee was a widow whose not too great income was derived from the interest on some four-per-cent. government bonds which represented the savings of her husband's life of toil, that was none the less hard because it was spent in a counting-room and not with shovel and spade. The coupon looked for all the world like a dollar bill, except that it was so small that a baby's hand could easily cover it. The United States, the printing on it said, would pay on demand to the bearer one dollar; and there was a number on it, just as on a full-grown dollar, that was the number of the bond from which it had been cut.

The letter traveled all night, and was tossed and sorted and bunched at the end of its journey in the great gray beehive that never sleeps, day or night, and where half the tears and joys of the land, including this account of the little dollar, are checked off unceasingly as first-class matter or second or third, as the case may be. In the morning it was laid, none the worse for its journey, at the professor's breakfast-plate. The professor was a kindly man, and he smiled as he read it. "To procure one small Christmas tree for a poor tenement," was its errand.

"Little dollar," he said, "I think I know where you are needed." And he made a note in his book. There were other notes there that made him smile again as he saw them. They had names set opposite them. One

about a Noah's ark was marked "Vivi."
That was the baby; and there was one about
a doll's carriage that had the words "Katie,
sure," set over against it. The professor
eyed the list in mock dismay.

"How ever will I do it?" he sighed, as he
put on his hat.

"Well, you will have to get Santa Claus
to help you, John," said his wife, buttoning
his greatcoat about him. "And, mercy! the
duckses' babies! don't forget them, whatever
you do. The baby has been talking about
nothing else since he saw them at the store,
the old duck and the two ducklings on
wheels. You know them, John?"

But the professor was gone, repeating to
himself as he went down the garden walk:
"The duckses' babies, indeed!" He chuckled
as he said it, why I cannot tell. He was
very particular about his grammar, was the
professor, ordinarily. Perhaps it was because it was Christmas eve.

Down-town went the professor; but instead of going with the crowd that was setting toward Santa Claus's headquarters, in
the big Broadway store, he turned off into a
quieter street, leading west. It took him to a
narrow thoroughfare, with five-story tene-

ments frowning on either side, where the
people he met were not so well dressed as
those he had left behind, and did not seem to
be in such a hurry of joyful anticipation of
the holiday. Into one of the tenements he
went, and, groping his way through a pitch-
dark hall, came to a door 'way back, the last
one to the left, at which he knocked. An
expectant voice said, "Come in," and the
professor pushed open the door.

The room was very small, very stuffy, and
very dark, so dark that a smoking kerosene-
lamp that burned on a table next the stove
hardly lighted it at all, though it was broad
day. A big, unshaven man, who sat on the
bed, rose when he saw the visitor, and stood
uncomfortably shifting his feet and avoiding
the professor's eye. The latter's glance was
serious, though not unkind, as he asked the
woman with the baby if he had found no
work yet.

"No," she said, anxiously coming to the
rescue, " not yet; he was waitin' for a recommend." But Johnnie had earned two dollars
running errands, and, now there was a big
fall of snow, his father might get a job of
shoveling. The woman's face was worried,
yet there was a cheerful note in her voice

that somehow made the place seem less discouraging than it was. The baby she nursed was not much larger than a middle-sized doll. Its little face looked thin and wan. It had been very sick, she explained, but the doctor said it was mending now. That was good, said the professor, and patted one of the bigger children on the head.

There were six of them, of all sizes, from Johnnie, who could run errands, down. They were busy fixing up a Christmas tree that half filled the room, though it was of the very smallest. Yes, it was a real Christmas tree, left over from the Sunday-school stock, and it was dressed up at that. Pictures from the colored supplement of a Sunday newspaper hung and stood on every branch, and three pieces of colored glass, suspended on threads that shone in the smoky lamplight, lent color and real beauty to the show. The children were greatly tickled.

"John put it up," said the mother, by way of explanation, as the professor eyed it approvingly. "There ain't nothing to eat on it. If there was, it would n't be there a minute. The childer be always a-searchin' in it."

"But there must be, or else it is n't a real Christmas tree," said the professor, and brought out the little dollar. "This is a dollar which a friend gave me for the children's Christmas, and she sends her love with it. Now, you buy them some things and a few candles, Mrs. Ferguson, and then a good supper for the rest of the family. Good night, and a Merry Christmas to you. I think myself the baby is getting better." It had just opened its eyes and laughed at the tree.

The professor was not very far on his way toward keeping his appointment with Santa Claus before Mrs. Ferguson was at the grocery laying in her· dinner. A dollar goes a long way when it is the only one in the house; and when she had everything, including two cents' worth of flitter-gold, four apples, and five candles for the.tree, the grocer footed up her bill on the bag that held her potatoes — ninety-eight cents.· Mrs. Ferguson gave him the little dollar.

"What 's this?" said the grocer, his fat smile turning cold as he laid a restraining hand on the full basket. "That ain't no good."

"It 's a dollar, ain't it?" said the woman, in alarm. "It 's all right. I know the man that give it to me."

"It ain't all right in this store," said the grocer, sternly. "Put them things back. I want none o' that."

The woman's eyes filled with tears as she slowly took the lid off the basket and lifted out the precious bag of potatoes. They were waiting for that dinner at home. The children were even then camping on the door-step to take her in to the tree in triumph. And now —

For the second time a restraining hand was laid upon her basket; but this time it was not the grocer's. A gentleman who had come in to order a Christmas turkey had overheard the conversation, and had seen the strange bill.

"It is all right," he said to the grocer. "Give it to me. Here is a dollar bill for it of the kind you know. If all your groceries were as honest as this bill, Mr. Schmidt, it would be a pleasure to trade with you. Don't be afraid to trust Uncle Sam where you see his promise to pay."

The gentleman held the door open for Mrs. Ferguson, and heard the shout of the delegation awaiting her on the stoop as he went down the street.

"I wonder where that came from, now," he

mused. "Coupons in Bedford street! I suppose somebody sent it to the woman for a Christmas gift. Hello! Here are old Thomas and Snowflake. I wonder if it would n't surprise her old stomach if I gave her a Christmas gift of oats. If only the shock does n't kill her! Thomas! Oh, Thomas!"

The old man thus hailed stopped and awaited the gentleman's coming. He was a cartman who did odd jobs through the ward, thus picking up a living for himself and the white horse, which the boys had dubbed Snowflake in a spirit of fun. They were a well-matched old pair, Thomas and his horse. One was not more decrepit than the other. There was a tradition along the docks, where Thomas found a job now and then, and Snowflake an occasional straw to lunch on, that they were of an age, but this was denied by Thomas.

"See here," said the gentleman, as he caught up with them; "I want Snowflake to keep Christmas, Thomas. Take this and buy him a bag of oats. And give it to him carefully, do you hear?—not all at once, Thomas. He is n't used to it."

"Gee whizz!" said the old man, rubbing his eyes with his cap, as his friend passed

out of sight, "oats fer Christmas! G'lang,
Snowflake; yer in luck."

The feed-man put on his spectacles and
looked Thomas over at the strange order.
Then he scanned the little dollar, first on one
side, then on the other.

"Never seed one like him," he said.
"'Pears to me he is mighty short. Wait till
I send round to the hockshop. He 'll know,
if anybody."

The man at the pawnshop did not need a
second look. "Why, of course," he said, and
handed a dollar bill over the counter. "Old
Thomas, did you say? Well, I am blamed if
the old man ain't got a stocking after all.
They 're a sly pair, he and Snowflake."

Business was brisk that day at the pawnshop. The door-bell tinkled early and late,
and the stock on the shelves grew. Bundle
was added to bundle. It had been a hard
winter so far. Among the callers in the
early afternoon was a young girl in a ging-
ham dress and without other covering, who
stood timidly at the counter and asked for
three dollars on a watch, a keepsake evidently, which she was loath to part with.
Perhaps it was the last glimpse of brighter
days. The pawnbroker was doubtful; it was

not worth so much. She pleaded hard, while he compared the number of the movement with a list sent in from Police Headquarters.

"Two," he said decisively at last, snapping the case shut—"two or nothing." The girl handed over the watch with a troubled sigh. He made out a ticket and gave it to her with a handful of silver change.

Was it the sigh and her evident distress, or was it the little dollar? As she turned to go, he called her back:

"Here, it is Christmas!" he said. "I 'll run the risk." And he added the coupon to the little heap.

The girl looked at it and at him questioningly.

"It is all right," he said; "you can take it; I 'm running short of change. Bring it back if they won't take it. I 'm good for it." Uncle Sam had achieved a backer.

In Grand street the holiday crowds jammed every store in their eager hunt for bargains. In one of them, at the knit-goods counter, stood the girl from the pawnshop, picking out a thick, warm shawl. She hesitated between a gray and a maroon-colored one, and held them up to the light.

"For you?" asked the salesgirl, thinking

to aid her. She glanced at her thin dress and shivering form as she said it.

"No," said the girl; "for mother; she is poorly and needs it." She chose the gray, and gave the salesgirl her handful of money.

The girl gave back the coupon.

"They don't go," she said; "give me another, please."

"But I have n't got another," said the girl, looking apprehensively at the shawl. "The —Mr. Feeney said it was all right. Take it to the desk, please, and ask."

The salesgirl took the bill and the shawl, and went to the desk. She came back, almost immediately, with the storekeeper, who looked sharply at the customer and noted the number of the coupon.

"It is all right," he said, satisfied apparently by the inspection; "a little unusual, only. We don't see many of them. Can I help you, miss?" And he attended her to the door.

In the street there was even more of a Christmas show going on than in the stores. Peddlers of toys, of mottos, of candles, and of knickknacks of every description stood in rows along the curb, and were driving a lively trade. Their push-carts were decorated with

fir-branches—even whole Christmas trees.
One held a whole cargo of Santa Clauses in
a bower of green, each one with a cedar-bush
in his folded arms, as a soldier carries his
gun. The lights were blazing out in the
stores, and the hucksters' torches were flaring at the corners. There was Christmas in
the very air and Christmas in the storekeeper's till. It had been a very busy day. He
thought of it with a satisfied nod as he stood
a moment breathing the brisk air of the
winter day, absently fingering the coupon
the girl had paid for the shawl. A thin voice
at his elbow said: "Merry Christmas, Mr.
Stein! Here 's yer paper."

It was the newsboy who left the evening
papers at the door every night. The storekeeper knew him, and something about the
struggle they had at home to keep the roof
over their heads. Mike was a kind of pro-
tégé of his. He had helped to get him his
route.

"Wait a bit, Mike," he said. "You 'll be
wanting your Christmas from me. Here 's a
dollar. It 's just like yourself: it is small,
but it is all right. You take it home and
have a good time."

Was it the message with which it had been
13

sent forth from far away in the country, or
what was it? Whatever it was, it was just
impossible for the little dollar to lie still in
the pocket while there was want to be relieved, mouths to be filled, or Christmas lights
to be lit. It just could n't, and it did n't.

Mike stopped around the corner of Allen
street, and gave three whoops expressive of
his approval of Mr. Stein ; having done which,
he sidled up to the first lighted window out
of range to examine his gift. His enthusiasm
changed to open-mouthed astonishment as
he saw the little dollar. His jaw fell. Mike
was not much of a scholar, and could not
make out the inscription on the coupon; but
he had heard of shin-plasters as something
they "had in the war," and he took this to
be some sort of a ten-cent piece. The policeman on the block might tell. Just now he
and Mike were hunk. They had made up
a little difference they 'd had, and if any
one would know, the cop surely would. And
off he went in search of him.

Mr. McCarthy pulled off his gloves, put his
club under his arm, and studied the little
dollar with contracted brow. He shook his
head as he handed it back, and rendered the
opinion that it was "some dom swindle that 's

ag'in' the law." He advised Mike to take it back to Mr. Stein, and added, as he prodded him in an entirely friendly manner in the ribs with his locust, that if it had been the week before he might have "run him in" for having the thing in his possession. As it happened, Mr. Stein was busy and not to be seen, and Mike went home between hope and fear, with his doubtful prize.

There was a crowd at the door of the tenement, and Mike saw, before he had reached it, running, that it clustered about an ambulance that was backed up to the sidewalk. Just as he pushed his way through the throng it drove off, its clanging gong scattering the people right and left. A little girl sat weeping on the top step of the stoop. To her Mike turned for information.

"Susie, what's up?" he asked, confronting her with his armful of papers. "Who's got hurted?"

"It's papa," sobbed the girl. "He ain't hurted. He's sick, and he was took that bad he had to go, an' to-morrer is Christmas, an' —oh, Mike!"

It is not the fashion of Essex street to slop over. Mike did n't. He just set his mouth to a whistle and took a turn down the hall to think. Susie was his chum. There were seven in her flat; in his only four, including two that made wages. He came back from his trip with his mind made up.

"Suse," he said, "come on in. You take this, Suse, see! an' let the kids have their Christmas. Mr. Stein give it to me. It 's a little one, but if it ain't all right I 'll take it back, and get one that is good. Go on, now, Suse, you hear?" And he was gone.

There was a Christmas tree that night in Susie's flat, with candles and apples and shining gold on, but the little dollar did not pay for it. That rested securely in the purse of the charity visitor who had come that afternoon, just at the right time, as it proved. She had heard the story of Mike and his sacrifice, and had herself given the children a one-dollar bill for the coupon. They had their Christmas, and a joyful one, too, for the lady went up to the hospital and brought back word that Susie's father would be all right with rest and care, which he was now getting. Mike came in and helped them "sack" the tree when the lady was gone. He gave three more whoops for Mr. Stein, three for the lady, and three for the hospital doctor to even things up. Essex street was all right that night.

"Do you know, professor," said that learned man's wife, when, after supper, he had settled down in his easy-chair to admire the Noah's ark and the duckses' babies and the rest, all of which had arrived safely by express ahead of him and were waiting to be detailed to their appropriate stockings while the children slept — "do you know, I heard such a story of a little newsboy to-day. It was at the meeting of our district charity committee this evening. Miss Linder, our visitor, came right from the house." And she told the story of Mike and Susie.

"And I just got the little dollar bill to keep. Here it is." She took the coupon out of her purse and passed it to her husband.

"Eh! what?" said the professor, adjusting his spectacles and reading the number. "If here is n't my little dollar come back to me! Why, where have you been, little one? I left you in Bedford street this morning, and here you come by way of Essex. Well, I declare!" And he told his wife how he had received it in a letter in the morning.

"John," she said, with a sudden impulse,—

she did n't know, and neither did he, that it was the charm of the little dollar that was working again, — "John, I guess it is a sin to stop it. Jones's children won't have any Christmas tree, because they can't afford it. He told me so this morning when he fixed the furnace. And the baby is sick. Let us give them the little dollar. He is here in the kitchen now."

And they did; and the Joneses, and I don't know how many others, had a Merry Christmas because of the blessed little dollar that carried Christmas cheer and good luck wherever it went. For all I know, it may be going yet. Certainly it is a sin to stop it, and if any one has locked it up without knowing that he locked up the Christmas dollar, let him start it right out again. He can tell it easily enough. If he just looks at the number, that 's the one.

A PROPOSAL ON THE ELEVATED

THE sleeper on the 3 : 35 A. M. elevated
train from the Harlem bridge was awake
for once. The sleeper is the last car in the
train, and has its own set that snores nightly
in the same seats, grunts with the fixed in-
hospitality of the commuter at the intrusion
of a stranger, and is on terms with Conrad,
the German conductor, who knows each one
of his passengers and wakes him up at his
station. The sleeper is unique. It is run for
the benefit of those who ride in it, not for the
company's. It not only puts them off properly; it waits for them, if they are not there.
The conductor knows that they will come.
They are men, mostly, with small homes beyond the bridge, whose work takes them
down-town to the markets, the Post-office, and
the busy marts of the city long before cock-

crow. The day begins in New York at all hours.

Usually the sleeper is all that its name implies, but this morning it was as far from it as could be. A party of young people, fresh from a neighborhood hop, had come on board and filled the rear end of the car. Their feet tripped yet to the dance, and snatches of the latest waltz floated through the train between peals of laughter and little girlish shrieks. The regulars glared, discontented, in strange seats, unable to go to sleep. Only the railroad yardmen dropped off promptly as they came in. Theirs was the shortest ride, and they could least afford to lose time. Two old Irishmen, flanked by their dinner-pails, gravely discussed the Henry George campaign.

Across the passage sat a group of three apart—a young man, a girl, and a little elderly woman with lines of care and hard work in her patient face. She guarded carefully three umbrellas, a very old and faded one, and two that were new and of silk, which she held in her lap, though it had not rained for a month. He was a likely young fellow, tall and straight, with the thoughtful eye of a student. His dark hair fell nearly to his shoulders, and his coat had a foreign cut.

The girl was a typical child of the city, slight
and graceful of form, dressed in good taste,
and with a bright, winning face. The two
chatted confidentially together, forgetful of
all else, while mama, between them, nodded
sleepily in her seat.

A sudden burst of white light flooded the
car.

"Hey! Ninety-ninth street!" called the
conductor, and rattled the door. The railroad
men tumbled out pell-mell, all but one. Conrad shook him, and he went out, mechanically
blinking his eyes.

"Eighty-ninth next!" from the doorway.

The laughter at the rear end of the car had
died out. The young people, in a quieter
mood, were humming a popular love-song.
Presently above the rest rose a clear tenor:

> Oh, promise me that some day you and I
> Will take our love together to some sky
> Where we can be alone and faith renew—

The clatter of the train as it flew over a
switch drowned the rest. When the last
wheel had banged upon the frog, I heard the
young student's voice, in the soft accents of
southern Europe:

"Wenn ich in Wien war—" He was telling her of his home and his people in the language of his childhood. I glanced across. She sat listening with kindling eyes. Mama slumbered sweetly; her worn old hands clutched unconsciously the umbrellas in her lap. The two Irishmen, having settled the campaign, had dropped to sleep, too. In the crowded car the two were alone. His hand sought hers and met it half-way.

"Forty-seventh!" There was a clatter of tin cans below. The contingent of milkmen scrambled out of their seats and off for the depot. In the lull that followed their going, the tenor rose from the last seat:

> Those first sweet violets of early spring,
> Which come in whispers, thrill us both, and sing
> Of love unspeakable that is to be,
> Oh, promise me! Oh, promise me!

The two young people faced each other. He had thrown his hat upon the seat beside him and held her hand fast, gesticulating with his free hand as he spoke rapidly, eloquently, eagerly of his prospects and his hopes. Her own toyed nervously with his coat-lapel, twisting and twirling a button as he went on. What he said might have been heard to the other end of the car, had there been anybody to listen. He was to live here always; his uncle would open a business in New York, of which he was to have charge, when he had learned to know the country and its people. It would not be long now, and then—and then—

"Twenty-third street!"

There was a long stop after the levy for the ferries had left. The conductor went out on the platform and consulted with the ticket-chopper. He was scrutinizing his watch for the second time, when the faint jingle of an east-bound car was heard.

"Here she comes!" said the ticket-chopper. A shout, and a man bounded up the steps, three at a time. It was an engineer who, to make connection with his locomotive at Chatham Square, must catch that train.

"Hullo, Conrad! Nearly missed you," he said as he jumped on the car, breathless.

"All right, Jack." And the conductor jerked the bell-rope. "You made it, though." The train sped on.

Two lives, heretofore running apart, were hastening to a union. The lovers had seen nothing, heard nothing but each other. His eyes burned as hers met his and fell before them. His head bent lower until his face al-

most touched hers.   His dark hair lay against
her blond curls.   The ostrich feather on her
hat swept his shoulder.

"Mögtest Du mich haben?" he entreated.

Above the grinding of the wheels as the
train slowed up for the station a block ahead,
pleaded the tenor:

> Oh, promise me that you will take my hand,
> The most unworthy in this lonely land—

Did she speak?   Her face was hidden, but
the blond curls moved with a nod so slight
that only a lover's eye could see it.   He seized
her disengaged hand.   The conductor stuck
his head into the car.

"Fourteenth street!"

A squad of stout, florid men with butchers'
aprons started for the door.   The girl arose
hastily.

"Mama!" she called, "steh' auf!   Es ist
Fourteenth street."

The little woman woke up, gathered the
umbrellas in her arms, and bustled after the
marketmen, her daughter leading the way.   He
sat as one dreaming.

"Ach!" he sighed, and ran his hand
through his dark hair, "so rasch!"

And he went out after them.

DEATH COMES TO CAT ALLEY

THE dead-wagon stopped at the mouth of Cat Alley. Its coming made a commotion among the children in the block, and the Chief of Police looked out of his window across the street, his attention arrested by the noise. He saw a little pine coffin carried into the alley under the arm of the driver, a shoal of ragged children trailing behind. After a while the driver carried it out again, shoved it in the wagon, where there were other boxes like it, and, slamming the door, drove off.

A red-eyed woman watched it down the street until it disappeared around the corner. Then she wiped her eyes with her apron and went in.

It was only Mary Welsh's baby that was dead, but to her the alley, never cheerful on

the brightest of days, seemed hopelessly deso-
late to-day. It was all she had. Her first
baby died in teething.

Cat Alley is a back-yard illustration of the
theory of evolution. The fittest survive, and
the Welsh babies were not among them. It
would be strange if they were. Mike, the
father, works in a Crosby-street factory when
he does work. It is necessary to put it that
way, for, though he has not been discharged,
he had only one day's work this week and
none at all last week. He gets one dollar a
day, and the one dollar he earned these last
two weeks his wife had to draw to pay the
doctor with when the baby was so sick. They
have had nothing else coming in, and but for
the wages of Mrs. Welsh's father, who lives
with them, there would have been nothing in
the house to eat.

The baby came three weeks ago, right in
the hardest of the hard times. It was never
strong enough to nurse, and the milk bought
in Mulberry street is not for babies to grow
on who are not strong enough to stand anything. Little John never grew at all. He
lay upon his pillow this morning as white
and wan and tiny as the day he came into a
world that did n't want him.

Yesterday, just before he died, he sat upon his grandmother's lap and laughed and crowed for the first time in his brief life, "just like he was talkin' to me," said the old woman, with a smile that struggled hard to keep down a sob. "I suppose it was a sort of inward cramp," she added—a mother's explanation of baby laugh in Cat Alley.

The mother laid out the little body on the only table in their room, in its only little white slip, and covered it with a piece of discarded lace curtain to keep off the flies. They had no ice, and no money to pay an undertaker for opening the little grave in Calvary, where their first baby lay. All night she sat by the improvised bier, her tears dropping silently.

When morning came and brought the woman with the broken arm from across the hall to sit by her, it was sadly evident that the burial of the child must be hastened. It was not well to look at the little face and the crossed baby hands, and even the mother saw it.

"Let the trench take him, in God's name; he has his soul," said the grandmother, crossing herself devoutly.

An undertaker had promised to put the

baby in the grave in Calvary for twelve dollars and take two dollars a week until it was paid. But how can a man raise two dollars a week, with only one coming in in two weeks, and that gone to the doctor? With a sigh Mike Welsh went for the "lines" that must smooth its way to the trench in the Potter's Field, and then to Mr. Blake's for the dead-wagon. It was the hardest walk of his life.

And so it happened that the dead-wagon halted at Cat Alley and that little John took his first and last ride. A little cross and a number on the pine box, cut in the lid with a chisel, and his brief history was closed, with only the memory of the little life remaining to the Welshes to help them fight the battle alone.

In the middle of the night, when the dead-lamp burned dimly at the bottom of the alley, a policeman brought to Police Headquarters a wailing child, an outcast found in the area of a Lexington-avenue house by a citizen, who handed it over to the police. Until its cries were smothered in the police nursery up-stairs with the ever-ready bottle, they reached the bereaved mother in Cat Alley and made her tears drop faster. As the dead-wagon drove

away with its load in the morning, Matron
Travers came out with the now sleeping waif
in her arms. She, too, was bound for Mr.
Blake's.

The two took their ride on the same boat
—the living child, whom no one wanted, to
Randall's Island, to be enlisted with its number in the army of the city's waifs, strong
and able to fight its way; the dead, for whom
a mother's heart yearns, to its place in the
great ditch.

WHY IT HAPPENED

YOM KIPPUR being at hand, all the East Side was undergoing a scrubbing, the people included. It is part of the religious observance of the chief Jewish holiday that every worshiper presenting himself at the synagogue to be cleansed from sin must first have washed his body clean.

Hence the numerous tenement bath-houses on the East Side are run night and day in Yom Kippur week to their full capacity. There are so many more people than tubs that there is no rest for the attendants even in the small hours of the morning.

They are not palatial establishments exactly, these *mikwehs* (bath-houses). Most of them are in keeping with the tenements that harbor them; but they fill the bill. One, at 20 Orchard street, has even a Turkish and a Russian attachment. It is one of the most pretentious. For thirty-five cents one can be roasted by dry heat or boiled with steam. The unhappy experience of Jacob Epstein shows that it is even possible to be boiled literally and in earnest in hot water at the same price. He chose that way unwittingly, and the choice came near causing a riot.

Epstein came to the bath-house with a party of friends at 2 A. M., in quest of a Russian bath. They had been steamed, and were disporting themselves to their heart's content when the thing befell the tailor. Epstein is a tailor. He went to get a shower-bath in a pail,—where Russian baths are got for thirty-five cents they are got partly by hand, as it were,—and in the dim, religious light of the room, the small gas-jet struggling ineffectually with the steam and darkness, he mistook the hot-water faucet for the cold. He found out his mistake when he raised the pail and poured a flood of boiling water over himself.

Then his shrieks filled the house. His companions paused in amazement, and beheld the tailor dancing on one foot and on the other by turns, yelling:

"Weh! Weh! Ich bin verbrennt!"

They thought he had gone suddenly mad, and joined in the lamentation, till one of them

saw his skin red and parboiled and raising
big blisters. Then they ran with a common
accord for their own cold-water pails, and pur-
sued him, seeking to dash their contents over
him.

But the tailor, frantic with pain, thought,
if he thought at all, that he was going to be
killed, and yelled louder than ever. His
companions' shouts, joined to his, were heard
in the street, and there promptly gathered
a wailing throng that echoed the "Weh!
Weh!" from within, and exchanged opinions
between their laments as to who was being
killed, and why.

Policeman Schulem came just in time to
prevent a general panic and restore peace.

Schulem is a valuable man on the East Side.
His name alone is enough. It signifies peace
—peace in the language of Ludlow street.
The crowd melted away, and the tailor was
taken to the hospital, bewailing his bad luck.

The bath-house keeper was an indignant
and injured man. His business was hurt.

"How did it happen?" he said. "It happened because he is a schlemiehl. *Teufel!* he's
worse than a schlemiehl; he is a chammer."

Which accounts for it, of course, and explains everything.

THE CHRISTENING IN BOTTLE ALLEY

ALL Bottle Alley was bidden to the christening. It being Sunday, when Mulberry street was wont to adjust its differences over the cards and the wine-cup, it came "heeled," ready for what might befall. From Tomaso, the rag-picker in the farthest rear cellar, to the Signor Undertaker, mainstay and umpire in the varying affairs of life, which had a habit in the Bend of lapsing suddenly upon his professional domain, they were all there, the men of Malpete's village. The baby was named for the village saint, so that it was a kind of communal feast as well. Carmen was there with her man, and Francisco Cessari.

If Carmen had any other name, neither Mulberry street nor the alley knew it. She was Carmen to them when, seven years before, she had taken up with Francisco, then a young mountaineer straight as the cedar of his native hills, the breath of which was yet in the songs with which he wooed her. Whether the priest had blessed their bonds no one knew or asked. The Bend only knew that one day, after three years during which the Francisco tenement had been the scene of more than one jealous quarrel, not, it was whispered, without cause, the mountaineer was missing. He did not come back. From over the sea the Bend heard, after a while, that he had reappeared in the old village to claim the sweetheart he had left behind. In the course of time new arrivals brought the news that Francisco was married and that they were living happily, as a young couple should. At the news Mulberry street looked askance at Carmen; but she gave no sign. By tacit consent, she was the Widow Carmen after that.

The summers passed. The fourth brought Francisco Cessari, come back to seek his fortune, with his wife and baby. He greeted old friends effusively and made cautious inquiries about Carmen. When told that she had consoled herself with his old rival, Luigi, with whom she was then living in Bottle

Alley, he laughed with a light heart, and took up his abode within half a dozen doors of the alley. That was but a short time before the christening at Malpete's. There their paths crossed each other for the first time since his flight.

She met him with a smile on her lips, but with hate in her heart. He, manlike, saw only the smile. The men smoking and drinking in the court watched them speak apart, saw him, with the laugh that sat so lightly upon his lips, turn to his wife, sitting by the hydrant with the child, and heard him say: "Look, Carmen! our baby!"

The woman bent over it, and, as she did, the little one woke suddenly out of its sleep and cried out in affright. It was noticed that Carmen smiled again then, and that the young mother shivered, why she herself could not have told. Francisco, joining the group at the farther end of the yard, said carelessly that she had forgotten. They poked fun at him and spoke Carmen's name loudly, with laughter.

From the tenement, as they did, came Luigi and asked threateningly who insulted his wife. They only laughed the more, said he had drunk too much wine, and, shoulder-

ing him out, bade him go look to his woman.
He went.   Carmen had witnessed it all from
the house.   She called him a coward and
goaded him with bitter taunts, until, mad with
anger and drink, he went out in the court
once more and shook his fist in the face of
Francisco.   They hailed his return with bantering words.   Luigi was spoiling for a fight,
they laughed, and would find one before the
day was much older.   But suddenly silence
fell upon the group.   Carmen stood on the
step, pale and cold.   She hid something under
her apron.

"Luigi!" she called, and he came to her.
She drew from under the apron a cocked pistol, and, pointing to Francisco, pushed it into
his hand.   At the sight the alley was cleared
as suddenly as if a tornado had swept through
it.   Malpete's guests leaped over fences, dived
into cellarways, anywhere for shelter.   The
door of the woodshed slammed behind Francisco just as his old rival reached it.   The
maddened man tore it open and dragged him
out by the throat.   He pinned him against
the fence, and leveled the pistol with frenzied
curses.   They died on his lips.   The face
that was turning livid in his grasp was the
face of his boyhood's friend.   They had gone

to school together, danced together at the
fairs in the old days. They had been friends
—till Carmen came. The muzzle of the
weapon fell.

"Shoot!" said a hard voice behind him.
Carmen stood there with face of stone. She
stamped her foot. "Shoot!" she commanded,
pointing, relentless, at the struggling man.
"Coward, shoot!"

Her lover's finger crooked itself upon the
trigger. A shriek, wild and despairing, rang
through the alley. A woman ran madly from
the house, flew across the pavement, and fell
panting at Carmen's feet.

"Mother of God! mercy!" she cried, thrust-
ing her babe before the assassin's weapon.
"Jesus Maria! Carmen, the child! He is my
husband!"

No gleam of pity came into the cold eyes.
Only hatred, fierce and bitter, was there. In
one swift, sweeping glance she saw it all: the
woman fawning at her feet, the man she hated
limp and helpless in the grasp of her lover.

"He was mine once," she said, "and he had
no mercy." She pushed the baby aside.
"Coward, shoot!"

The shot was drowned in the shriek, hopeless, despairing, of the widow who fell upon

the body of Francisco as it slipped lifeless from the grasp of the assassin. The christening party saw Carmen standing over the three with the same pale smile on her cruel lips.

For once the Bend did not shield a murderer. The door of the tenement was shut against him. The women spurned him. The very children spat at him as he fled to the street. The police took him there. With him they seized Carmen. She made no attempt to escape. She had bided her time, and it had come. She had her revenge. To the end of its lurid life Bottle Alley remembered it as the murder accursed of God.

IN THE MULBERRY STREET COURT

"CONDUCT unbecoming an officer," read the charge, " in this, to wit, that the said defendants brought into the station-house, by means to deponent unknown, on the said Fourth of July, a keg of beer, and, when apprehended, were consuming the contents of the same." Twenty policemen, comprising the whole off platoon of the East One Hundred and Fourth street squad, answered the charge as defendants. They had been caught grouped about a pot of chowder and the fatal keg in the top-floor dormitory, singing, " Beer, beer, glorious beer ! " Sergeant McNally and Roundsman Stevenson interrupted the proceedings.

The commissioner's eyes bulged as, at the call of the complaint clerk, the twenty marched up and ranged themselves in rows, three deep, before him.

They took the oath collectively, with a toss and a smack, as if to say, "I don't care if I do," and told separately and identically the same story, while the sergeant stared and the commissioner's eyes grew bigger and rounder.

Missing his reserves, Sergeant McNally had sent the roundsman in search of them. He was slow in returning, and the sergeant went on a tour of inspection himself. He journeyed to the upper region, and there came upon the party in full swing. Then and there he called the roll. Not one of the platoon was missing.

They formed a hollow square around something that looked uncommonly like a beer-keg. A number of tin growlers stood beside it. The sergeant picked up one and turned the tap. There was enough left in the keg to barely half fill it. Seeing that, the platoon followed him down-stairs without a murmur.

One by one the twenty took the stand after the sergeant had left it, and testified without a tremor that they had seen no beer-keg. In fact, the majority would not know one if they saw it. They were tired and hungry, having been held in reserve all day, when a pleasant smell assailed their nostrils.

Each of the twenty followed his nose independently to the top floor, where he was surprised to see the rest gathered about a pot of steaming chowder. He joined the circle and partook of some. It was good. As to beer, he had seen none and drunk less. There was something there of wood with a brass handle to it. What it was none of them seemed to know. They were all shocked at the idea that it might have been a beer-keg. Such things are forbidden in police stations.

The sergeant himself could not tell how it could have got in there, while stoutly maintaining that it was a keg. He scratched his head and concluded that it might have come over the roof or, somehow, from a building that is in course of erection next door. The chowder had come in by the main door. At least, one policeman had seen it carried upstairs. He had fallen in behind it immediately.

When the commissioner had heard this story told exactly twenty times the platoon fell in and marched off to the elevated station. When he can decide what punishment to inflict on a policeman who does not know a beer-keg when he sees it, they all will be fined accordingly, and a door-man who has served a term as a barkeeper will be sent to the East One Hundred and Fourth street station to keep the police there out of harm's way.

SPOONING IN DYNAMITE ALLEY

D YNAMITE ALLEY is bereft. Its spring
spooning is over. Once more the growler
has the right of way. But what good is it,
with Kate Cassidy hiding in her third floor
back, her "steady" hiding from the police,
and Tom Hart laid up in hospital with two of
his "slats stove in," all along of their "spiel-
ing"? There will be nothing now to heave a
brick at on a dark night, and no chance for
a row for many a day to come. No wonder
Dynamite Alley is out of sorts.

It got its name from the many rows that
traveled in the wake of the growler out and
in at the three-foot gap between brick walls,
which was a garden walk when the front
house was young and pansies and spiderwort
grew in the back lot. These many years a
tenement has stood there, and as it grew

223

older and more dilapidated, rows multiplied and grew noisier, until the explosive name was hooked to the alley by the neighbors, and stuck. It was long after that that the Cassidys, father and daughter, came to live in it, and also the Harts. Their coming wrought no appreciable change, except that it added another and powerful one to the dynamic forces of the alley—jealousy. Kate is pretty. She is blonde and she is twenty. She greases plates in a pie bakery in Sullivan street by day, and so earns her own living. Of course she is a favorite. There is n't a ball going on that she does n't attend, or a picnic either. It was at one of them, the last of the Hounds' balls, that she met George Finnegan.

There were n't many hours after that when they did n't meet. He made the alley his headquarters by day and by night. On the morning after the ball he scandalized it by spooning with Kate from daybreak till nine o'clock. By the middle of the afternoon he was back again, and all night, till every one was asleep, he and Kate held the alley by main strength, as it were, the fact being that when they were in it no one could pass. Their spooning blocked it, blocked the way

of the growler.   The alley called it mean, and
trouble began promptly.

After that things fell by accident out of the
windows of the rear tenement when Kate and
George Finnegan were sitting in the doorway.
They tried to reduce the chances of a hit as
much as might be by squeezing into the space
of one, at which the alley jeered.   Sometimes
one of the tenants would jostle them in the
yard and "give lip," in the alley's vernacular,
and Kate would retort with dignity: "Excuse yerself.   Ye don't know who yer talkin'
to."

It had to come to it, and it did.   Finnegan
had been continuing the siege since the warm
weather set in.   He was a good spieler, Kate
gave in to that.   But she had n't taken him
for her steady yet, though the alley let on
it thought so.   Her steady is away at sea.
George evidently thought the time ripe for
cutting him out.   His spooning ran into the
small hours of the morning, night after night.

It was near 1 A. M. that morning when
Thomas Hart came down to the yard, stumbled over the pair in the doorway, and made
remarks.   As he passed out of sight, George,
the swain, said:

"If he gives any more lip when he comes

15

back, I 'll swing on him." And just then Hart
came back.

He did " give lip," and George "swung on
him." It took him in the eye, and he fell.
Then he jumped on him and stove in his
slats. Kate ran.

After all, George Finnegan was not game.
When Hart's wife came down to see who
groaned in the yard, and, finding her husband, let out those blood-curdling yells which
made Kate Cassidy hide in an ice-wagon half-
way down the block, he deserted Kate and ran.

Mistress Hart's yells brought Policeman
Devery. He did n't ask whence they came,
but made straight for the alley. Mistress
Hart was there, vowing vengeance upon
" Kate Cassidy's feller," who had done up her
man. She vowed vengeance in such a loud
voice that the alley trembled with joyful
excitement, while Kate, down the street, crept
farther into the ice-wagon, trembling also,
but with fear. Kate is not a fighter. She is
too good-looking for that.

The policeman found her there and escorted
her home, past the Hart door, after he had
sent Mister Hart to the hospital, where the
doctors fixed his slats (ribs, that is to say).
Mistress Hart, outnumbered, fell back and

organized an ambush, vowing that she would lay Kate out yet. Discovering that the Floods, next door, had connived at her enemy's descent by way of their fire-escape, she included them in the siege by prompt declaration of war upon the whole floor.

The cause of it all, safe in the bakery, suspended the greasing of pie-plates long enough to give her version of the row:

"We were a-sittin' there, quiet an' peaceful like," she said, "when Mister Hart came along an' made remarks, an' George he give it back to him good. 'Oh,' says he, 'you ain't a thousand; yer only one,' an' he went. When he came back, George he stood up, an' Mister Hart he says to me: 'Ye 're not an up-stairs girl; you can be called down,' an' George he up an' struck him. I did n't wait fer no more. I just run out of the alley. Is he hurted bad?

"Who is George? He is me feller. I met him at the Hounds' ball in Germania Hall, an' he treated me same as you would any lady. We danced together an' had a couple of drinks, an' he took me home. George ain't me steady, you know. Me regular he is to sea. See?

"I did n't see nothin'. I hid in the wagon

while I heard him callin' names. I was n't goin' in till Mr. Deevy [Policeman Devery] he came along. I told him I was scart, and he said: 'Oh, come along.' But I was dead scart.

"Say, you won't forget to come to our picnic, the 'Pie-Girls,' will you? It 'll be great."

HEROES WHO FIGHT FIRE

THIRTEEN years have passed since, but it is all to me as if it had happened yesterday—the clanging of the fire-bells, the hoarse shouts of the firemen, the wild rush and terror of the streets; then the great hush that fell upon the crowd; the sea of upturned faces, with the fire-glow upon it; and up there, against the background of black smoke that poured from roof and attic, the boy clinging to the narrow ledge, so far up that it seemed humanly impossible that help could ever come.

But even then it was coming. Up from the street, while the crew of the truck company were laboring with the heavy extension-ladder that at its longest stretch was many feet too short, crept four men upon long, slender poles with cross-bars, iron-hooked at the end.   Standing in one window, they reached up and thrust the hook through the next one above, then mounted a story higher. Again the crash of glass, and again the dizzy ascent.   Straight up the wall they crept, looking like human flies on the ceiling, and clinging as close, never resting, reaching one recess only to set out for the next; nearer and nearer in the race for life, until but a single span separated the foremost from the boy. And now the iron hook fell at his feet, and the fireman stood upon the step with the res- cued lad in his arms, just as the pent-up flame burst lurid from the attic window, reaching with impotent fury for its prey. The next moment they were safe upon the great ladder waiting to receive them below.

Then such a shout went up!   Men fell on each other's necks, and cried and laughed at once.   Strangers slapped one another on the back, with glistening faces, shook hands, and behaved generally like men gone suddenly mad.   Women wept in the street.   The driver of a car stalled in the crowd, who had stood through it all speechless, clutching the reins, whipped his horses into a gallop, and drove away yelling like a Comanche, to relieve his feelings.   The boy and his rescuer were car-

ried across the street without any one knowing how. Policemen forgot their dignity,
and shouted with the rest. Fire, peril, terror,
and loss were alike forgotten in the one touch
of nature that makes the whole world kin.

Fireman John Binns was made captain of
his crew, and the Bennett medal was pinned
on his coat on the next parade-day. The
burning of the St. George Flats was the first
opportunity New York had of witnessing a
rescue with the scaling-ladders that form such
an essential part of the equipment of the fire-
fighters to-day. Since then there have been
many such. In the company in which John
Binns was a private of the second grade, two
others to-day bear the medal for brave deeds:
the foreman, Daniel J. Meagher, and Private
Martin M. Coleman, whose name has been
seven times inscribed on the roll of honor for
twice that number of rescues, any one of
which stamped him as a man among men, a
real hero. And Hook-and-Ladder No. 3 is
not specially distinguished among the fire-
crews of the metropolis for daring and courage. New-Yorkers are justly proud of their
firemen. Take it all in all, there is not, I
think, to be found anywhere a body of men
as fearless, as brave, and as efficient as the

Fire Brigade of New York. I have known it well for twenty years, and I speak from a personal acquaintance with very many of its men, and from a professional knowledge of more daring feats, more hairbreadth escapes, and more brilliant work, than could well be recorded between the covers of this book.

Indeed, it is hard, in recording any, to make a choice, and to avoid giving the impression that recklessness is a chief quality in the fireman's make-up. That would not be true. His life is too full of real peril for him to expose it recklessly—that is to say, needlessly. From the time when he leaves his quarters in answer to an alarm until he returns, he takes a risk that may at any moment set him face to face with death in its most cruel form. He needs nothing so much as a clear head; and nothing is prized so highly, nothing puts him so surely in the line of promotion; for as he advances in rank and responsibility, the lives of others, as well as his own, come to depend on his judgment. The act of conspicuous daring which the world applauds is oftenest to the fireman a matter of simple duty that had to be done in that way because there was no other. Nor is it always, or even usually, the hardest duty, as he sees it. It came easy to him because he is an athlete trained to do just such things, and because once for all it is easier to risk one's life in the open, in the sight of one's fellows, than to face death alone, caught like a rat in a trap. That is the real peril which he knows too well; but of that the public hears only when he has fought his last fight, and lost.

How literally our every-day security—of which we think, if we think of it at all, as a mere matter of course—is built upon the supreme sacrifice of these devoted men, we realize at long intervals, when a disaster occurs such as the one in which Chief Bresnan and Foreman Rooney[1] lost their lives three years ago. They were crushed to death under the great water-tank in a Twenty-fourth street factory that was on fire. Its supports had been burned away. An examination that was then made of the water-tanks in the city discovered eight thousand that were either

[1] Rooney wore the Bennett medal for saving the life of a woman at the disastrous fire in the old "World" building, on January 31, 1882. The ladder upon which he stood was too short. Riding upon the topmost rung, he bade the woman jump, and caught and held her as she fell.

wholly unsupported, except by the roof-beams, or propped on timbers, and therefore a direct menace, not only to the firemen when they were called there, but daily to those living under them. It is not pleasant to add that the department's just demand for a law that should compel landlords either to build tanks on the wall or on iron supports has not been heeded yet; but that is, unhappily, an old story.

Seventeen years ago the collapse of a Broadway building during a fire convinced the community that stone pillars were unsafe as supports. The fire was in the basement, and the firemen had turned the hose on. When the water struck the hot granite columns, they cracked and fell, and the building fell with them. There were upon the roof at the time a dozen men of the crew of Truck Company No. 1, chopping holes for smoke-vents. The majority clung to the parapet, and hung there till rescued. Two went down into the furnace from which the flames shot up twenty feet when the roof broke. One, Fireman Thomas J. Dougherty, was a wearer of the Bennett medal, too. His foreman answers on parade-day, when his name is called, that he "died on the field of duty." These, at all

events, did not die in vain. Stone columns
are not now used as supports for buildings in
New York.

So one might go on quoting the perils of
the firemen as so many steps forward for the
better protection of the rest of us. It was
the burning of the St. George Flats, and more
recently of the Manhattan Bank, in which a
dozen men were disabled, that stamped the
average fire-proof construction as faulty
and largely delusive. One might even go
further, and say that the fireman's risk increases in the ratio of our progress or con-
venience. The water-tanks came with the
very high buildings, which in themselves offer
problems to the fire-fighters that have not
yet been solved. The very air-shafts that
were hailed as the first advance in tenement-house building added enormously to the
fireman's work and risk, as well as to the
risk of every one dwelling under their roofs,
by acting as so many huge chimneys that
carried the fire to the windows opening upon
them in every story. More than half of all
the fires in New York occur in tenement-
houses. When the Tenement-House Com-
mission of 1894 sat in this city, considering
means of making them safer and better, it

received the most practical help and advice from the firemen, especially from Chief Bresnan, whose death occurred only a few days after he had testified as a witness. The recommendations upon which he insisted are now part of the general tenement-house law.

Chief Bresnan died leading his men against the enemy. In the Fire Department the battalion chief leads; he does not direct operations from a safe position in the rear. Perhaps this is one of the secrets of the indomitable spirit of his men. Whatever hardships they have to endure, his is the first and the biggest share. Next in line comes the captain, or foreman, as he is called. Of the six who were caught in the fatal trap of the water-tank, four hewed their way out with axes through an intervening partition. They were of the ranks. The two who were killed were the chief and Assistant Foreman John L. Rooney, who was that day in charge of his company, Foreman Shaw having just been promoted to Bresnan's rank. It was less than a year after that Chief Shaw was killed in a fire in Mercer street. I think I could reckon up as many as five or six battalion chiefs who have died in that way, leading their men. They would not deserve the name if they did not follow such leaders, no matter where the road led.

In the chief's quarters of the Fourteenth Battalion up in Wakefield there sits to-day a man, still young in years, who in his maimed body but unbroken spirit bears such testimony to the quality of New York's fire-fighters as the brave Bresnan and his comrade did in their death.   Thomas J. Ahearn led his company as captain to a fire in the Consolidated Gas-Works on the East Side.   He found one of the buildings ablaze.   Far toward the rear, at the end of a narrow lane, around which the fire swirled and arched itself, white and wicked, lay the body of a man—dead, said the panic-stricken crowd.   His sufferings had been brief.   A worse fate threatened all unless the fire was quickly put out.   There were underground   reservoirs   of   naphtha—the ground was honeycombed with them—that might explode at any moment with the fire raging overhead.   The peril was instant and great.   Captain Ahearn looked at the body, and saw it stir.   The watch-chain upon the man's vest rose and fell as if he were breathing.

"He is not dead," he said.   "I am going to get that man out."   And he crept down the lane of fire, unmindful of the hidden dangers, seeing only the man who was perishing. The flames scorched him; they blocked his way; but he came through alive, and brought out his man, so badly hurt, however, that he died in the hospital that day. The Board of Fire Commissioners gave Ahearn the medal for bravery, and made him chief. Within a year he all but lost his life in a gallant attempt to save the life of a child that was supposed to be penned in a burning Rivington-street tenement. Chief Ahearn's quarters were near by, and he was first on the ground. A desperate man confronted him in the hallway. "My child! my child!" he cried, and wrung his hands. "Save him! He is in there." He pointed to the back room. It was black with smoke. In the front room the fire was raging. Crawling on hands and feet, the chief made his way into the room the man had pointed out. He groped under the bed, and in it, but found no child there. Satisfied that it had escaped, he started to return. The smoke had grown so thick that breathing was no longer possible, even at the floor. The chief drew his coat over his head, and made a dash for the hall door. He reached it only to find that the spring-lock had snapped shut.

The door-knob burned his hand. The fire burst through from the front room, and seared his face. With a last effort, he kicked the lower panel out of the door, and put his head through. And then he knew no more.

His men found him lying so when they came looking for him. The coat was burned off his back, and of his hat only the wire rim remained. He lay ten months in the hospital, and came out deaf and wrecked physically. At the age of forty-five the board retired him to the quiet of the country district, with this formal resolution, that did the board more credit than it could do him. It is the only one of its kind upon the department books:

Resolved, That in assigning Battalion Chief Thomas J. Ahearn to command the Fourteenth Battalion, in the newly annexed district, the Board deems it proper to express the sense of obligation felt by the Board and all good citizens for the brilliant and meritorious services of Chief Ahearn in the discharge of duty which will always serve as an example and an inspiration to our uniformed force, and to express the hope that his future years of service at a less arduous post may be as comfortable and pleasant as his former years have been brilliant and honorable.

Firemen are athletes as a matter of course. They have to be, or they could not hold their places for a week, even if they could get into them at all. The mere handling of the scaling-ladders, which, light though they seem, weigh from sixteen to forty pounds, requires unusual strength. No particular skill is needed. A man need only have steady nerve, and the strength to raise the long pole by its narrow end, and jam the iron hook through a window which he cannot see but knows is there. Once through, the teeth in the hook and the man's weight upon the ladder hold it safe, and there is no real danger unless he loses his head. Against that possibility the severe drill in the school of instruction is the barrier. Any one to whom climbing at dizzy heights, or doing the hundred and one things of peril to ordinary men which firemen are constantly called upon to do, causes the least discomfort, is rejected as unfit. About five per cent. of all appointees are eliminated by the ladder test, and never get beyond their probation service. A certain smaller percentage takes itself out through loss of "nerve" generally. The first experience of a room full of smothering smoke, with the fire roaring overhead, is generally sufficient to convince the timid that the service is not for him. No cowards are dismissed from the department, for the reason that none get into it.

The notion that there is a life-saving corps apart from the general body of firemen rests upon a mistake. They are one. Every fireman nowadays must pass muster at life-saving drill, must climb to the top of any building on his scaling-ladder, slide down with a rescued comrade, or jump without hesitation from the third story into the life-net spread below. By such training the men are fitted for their work, and the occasion comes soon that puts them to the test. It came to Daniel J. Meagher, of whom I spoke as foreman of Hook-and-Ladder Company No. 3, when, in the midnight hour, a woman hung from the fifth-story window of a burning building, and the longest ladder at hand fell short ten or a dozen feet of reaching her. The boldest man in the crew had vainly attempted to get to her, and in the effort had sprained his foot. There were no scaling-ladders then. Meagher ordered the rest to plant the ladder on the stoop and hold it out from the building so that he might reach the very topmost step. Balanced thus where the slightest tremor might have caused ladder and all to crash to the ground, he bade the woman drop, and receiving her in his arms, carried her down safe.

16

No one but an athlete with muscles and nerves of steel could have performed such a feat, or that which made Dennis Ryer, of the crew of Engine No. 36, famous three years ago. That was on Seventh Avenue at One Hundred and Thirty-fourth street. A flat was on fire, and the tenants had fled; but one, a woman, bethought herself of her parrot, and went back for it, to find escape by the stairs cut off when she again attempted to reach the street. With the parrot-cage, she appeared at the top-floor window, framed in smoke, calling for help. Again there was no ladder to reach. There were neighbors on the roof with a rope, but the woman was too frightened to use it herself. Dennis Ryer made it fast about his own waist, and bade the others let him down, and hold on for life. He drew the woman out, but she was heavy, and it was all they could do above to hold them. To pull them over the cornice was out of the question. Upon the highest step of the ladder, many feet below, stood Ryer's father, himself a fireman of another company, and saw his boy's peril.

"Hold fast, Dennis!" he shouted. "If you fall I will catch you." Had they let go, all three would have been killed. The young

fireman saw the danger, and the one door of
escape, with a glance. The window before
which he swung, half smothered by the smoke
that belched from it, was the last in the house.
Just beyond, in the window of the adjoining
house, was safety, if he could but reach it.
Putting out a foot, he kicked the wall, and
made himself swing toward it, once, twice,
bending his body to add to the motion. The
third time he all but passed it, and took a
mighty grip on the affrighted woman, shouting
into her ear to loose her own hold at the same
time. As they passed the window on the
fourth trip, he thrust her through sash and
all with a supreme effort, and himself followed
on the next rebound, while the street, that
was black with a surging multitude, rang
with a mighty cheer. Old Washington Ryer,
on his ladder, threw his cap in the air, and
cheered louder than all the rest. But the
parrot was dead—frightened to death, very
likely, or smothered.

I once asked Fireman Martin M. Coleman,
after one of those exhibitions of coolness and
courage that thrust him constantly upon
the notice of the newspaper man, what he
thought of when he stood upon the ladder,
with this thing before him to do that might

mean life or death the next moment. He
looked at me in some perplexity.

"Think?" he said slowly. "Why, I don't
think. There ain't any time to. If I'd
stopped to think, them five people would 'a'
been burnt. No; I don't think of danger. If
it is anything, it is that—up there—I am boss.
The rest are not in it. Only I wish," he added,
rubbing his arm ruefully at the recollection,
"that she had n't fainted. It 's hard when
they faint. They 're just so much dead-
weight. We get no help at all from them
heavy women."

And that was all I could get out of him. I
never had much better luck with Chief Benjamin A. Gicquel, who is the oldest wearer of
the Bennett medal, just as Coleman is the
youngest, or the one who received it last. He
was willing enough to talk about the science
of putting out fires; of Department Chief
Bonner, the "man of few words," who, he
thinks, has mastered the art beyond any man
living; of the back-draft, and almost anything
else pertaining to the business: but when I
insisted upon his telling me the story of the
rescue of the Schaefer family of five from a
burning tenement down in Cherry street, in
which he earned his rank and reward, he

laughed a good-humored little laugh, and said that it was "the old man"—meaning Schaefer—who should have had the medal. "It was a grand thing in him to let the little ones come out first." I have sometimes wished that firemen were not so modest. It would be much easier, if not so satisfactory, to record their gallant deeds. But I am not sure that it is, after all, modesty so much as a wholly different point of view. It is business with them, the work of their lives. The one feeling that is allowed to rise beyond this is the feeling of exultation in the face of peril conquered by courage, which Coleman expressed. On the ladder he was boss! It was the fancy of a masterful man, and none but a masterful man would have got upon the ladder at all.

Doubtless there is something in the spectacular side of it that attracts. It would be strange if there were not. There is everything in a fireman's existence to encourage it. Day and night he leads a kind of hair-trigger life, that feeds naturally upon excitement, even if only as a relief from the irksome idling in quarters. Try as they may to give him enough to do there, the time hangs heavily upon his hands, keyed up as he is, and need be, to adventurous deeds at shortest notice. He falls to grumbling and quarreling, and the necessity becomes imperative of holding him to the strictest discipline, under which he chafes impatiently. "They nag like a lot of old women," said Department Chief Bonner to me once; "and the best at a fire are often the worst in the house." In the midst of it all the gong strikes a familiar signal. The horses' hoofs thunder on the planks; with a leap the men go down the shining pole to the main floor, all else forgotten; and with crash and clatter and bang the heavy engine swings into the street, and races away on a wild gallop, leaving a trail of fire behind.

Presently the crowd sees rubber-coated, helmeted men with pipe and hose go through a window from which such dense smoke pours forth that it seems incredible that a human being could breathe it for a second and live. The hose is dragged squirming over the sill, where shortly a red-eyed face with disheveled hair appears, to shout something hoarsely to those below, which they understand. Then, unless some emergency arise, the spectacular part is over. Could the citizen whose heart beat as he watched them

enter see them now, he would see grimy
shapes, very unlike the fine-looking men who
but just now had roused his admiration,
crawling on hands and knees, with their noses
close to the floor if the smoke be very dense,
ever pointing the "pipe" in the direction
where the enemy is expected to appear.   The
fire is the enemy; but he can fight that, once
he reaches it, with something of a chance.
The smoke kills without giving him a show
to fight back.   Long practice toughens him
against it, until he learns the trick of "eating
the smoke."   He can breathe where a candle
goes out for want of oxygen.   By holding his
mouth close to the nozzle, he gets what little
air the stream of water brings with it and sets
free; and within a few inches of the floor there
is nearly always a current of air.   In the last
emergency, there is the hose that he can follow out.   The smoke always is his worst
enemy.   It lays ambushes for him which he
can suspect, but not ward off.   He tries to, by
opening vents in the roof as soon as the pipe-
men are in place and ready; but in spite of
all precautions, he is often surprised by the
dreaded back-draft.

I remember standing in front of a burning
Broadway store, one night, when the back-

draft blew out the whole front without warning. It is simply an explosion of gases generated by the heat, which must have vent, and go upon the line of least resistance, up, or down, or in a circle—it does not much matter, so that they go. It swept shutters, windows, and all, across Broadway, in this instance, like so much chaff, littering the street with heavy rolls of cloth. The crash was like a fearful clap of thunder. Men were knocked down on the opposite sidewalk, and two teams of engine horses, used to almost any kind of happening at a fire, ran away in a wild panic. It was a blast of that kind that threw down and severely injured Battalion Chief M'Gill, one of the oldest and most experienced of firemen, at a fire on Broadway in March, 1890; and it has cost more brave men's lives than the fiercest fire that ever raged. The "puff," as the firemen call it, comes suddenly, and from the corner where it is least expected. It is dread of that, and of getting overcome by the smoke generally, which makes firemen go always in couples or more together. They never lose sight of one another for an instant, if they can help it. If they do, they go at once in search of the lost.

The delay of a moment may prove fatal to him.

Lieutenant Samuel Banta of the Franklin-street company, discovering the pipe that had just been held by Fireman Quinn at a Park-Place fire thrashing aimlessly about, looked about him, and saw Quinn floating on his face in the cellar, which was running full of water. He had been overcome, had tumbled in, and was then drowning, with the fire raging above and alongside. Banta jumped in after him, and endeavored to get his head above water. While thus occupied, he glanced up, and saw the preliminary puff of the backdraft bearing down upon him. The lieutenant dived at once, and tried to pull his unhappy pipe-man with him; but he struggled and worked himself loose. From under the water Banta held up a hand, and it was burnt. He held up the other, and knew that the puff had passed when it came back unsinged. Then he brought Quinn out with him; but it was too late. Caught between flood and fire, he had no chance. When I asked the lieutenant about it, he replied simply: "The man in charge of the hose fell into the cellar. I got him out; that was all."

"But how?" I persisted. "Why, I went down through the cellar," said the lieutenant, smiling, as if it was the most ordinary thing in the world.

It was this same Banta who, when Fireman David H. Soden had been buried under the falling walls of a Pell-street house, crept through a gap in the basement wall, in among the fallen timbers, and, in imminent peril of his own life, worked there with a hand-saw two long hours to free his comrade, while the firemen held the severed timbers up with ropes to give him a chance. Repeatedly, while he was at work, his clothes caught fire, and it was necessary to keep playing the hose upon him. But he brought out his man safe and sound, and, for the twentieth time perhaps, had his name recorded on the roll of merit. His comrades tell how, at one of the twenty, the fall of a building in Hall Place had left a workman lying on a shaky piece of wall, helpless, with a broken leg. It could not bear the weight of a ladder, and it seemed certain death to attempt to reach him, when Banta, running up a slanting beam that still hung to its fastening with one end, leaped from perch to perch upon the wall, where hardly a goat could have found footing, reached his man, and brought him down slung over his shoulder, and swearing at him like a trooper lest the peril of the descent cause him to lose his nerve and with it the lives of both.

Firemen dread cellar fires more than any other kind, and with reason. It is difficult to make a vent for the smoke, and the danger of drowning is added to that of being smothered when they get fairly to work. If a man is lost to sight or touch of his fellows there for ever so brief a while, there are five chances to one that he will not again be seen alive. Then there ensues such a fight as the city witnessed only last May at the burning of a Chambers-street paper-warehouse. It was fought out deep underground, with fire and flood, freezing cold and poisonous gases, leagued against Chief Bonner's forces. Next door was a cold-storage house, whence the cold. Something that was burning—I do not know that it was ever found out just what— gave forth the smothering fumes before which the firemen went down in squads. File after file staggered out into the street, blackened and gasping, to drop there. The near engine-house was made into a hospital, where the senseless men were laid on straw hastily spread. Ambulance surgeons worked over them. As fast as they were brought to, they went back to bear a hand in the work of rescue. In delirium they fought to return. Down in the depths one of their number was lying helpless.

There is nothing finer in the records of glorious war than the story of the struggle these brave fellows kept up for hours against tremendous odds for the rescue of their comrade. Time after time they went down into the pit of deadly smoke, only to fail. Lieutenant Banta tried twice and failed. Fireman King was pulled up senseless, and having been brought round, went down once more. Fireman Sheridan returned empty-handed, more dead than alive. John O'Connell, of Truck No. 1, at length succeeded in reaching his comrade and tying a rope about him, while from above they drenched both with water to keep them from roasting. They drew up a dying man; but John G. Reinhardt dead is more potent than a whole crew of firemen alive. The story of the fight for his life will long be told in the engine-houses of New York, and will nerve the Kings and the Sheridans and the O'Connells of another day to like deeds.

How firemen manage to hear in their

sleep the right signal, while they sleep right through any number that concerns the next company, not them, is one of the mysteries that will probably always remain unsolved. "I don't know," said Department Chief Bonner, when I asked him once. "I guess it is the same way with everybody. You hear what you have to hear. There is a gong right over my bed at home, and I hear every stroke of it, but I don't hear the baby. My wife hears the baby if it as much as stirs in its crib, but not the gong." Very likely he is right. The fact that the fireman can hear and count correctly the strokes of the gong in his sleep has meant life to many hundreds, and no end of property saved; for it is in the early moments of a fire that it can be dealt with summarily. I recall one instance in which the failure to interpret a signal properly, or the accident of taking a wrong road to the fire, cost a life, and, singularly enough, that of the wife of one of the firemen who answered the alarm. It was all so pitiful, so tragic, that it has left an indelible impression on my mind. It was the fire at which Patrick F. Lucas earned the medal for that year by snatching five persons. out of the very jaws of death in a Dominick-street tenement. The alarm-signal rang in the hook-and-ladder company's quarters in North Moore street, but was either misunderstood or they made a wrong start. Instead of turning east to West Broadway, the truck turned west, and went galloping toward Greenwich street. It was only a few seconds, the time that was lost, but it was enough. Fireman Murphy's heart went up in his throat when, from his seat on the truck as it flew toward the fire, he saw that it was his own home that was burning. Up on the fifth floor he found his wife penned in. She died in his arms as he carried her to the fire-escape. The fire, for once, had won in the race for a life.

While I am writing this, the morning paper that is left at my door tells the story of a fireman who, laid up with a broken ankle in an up-town hospital, jumped out of bed, forgetting his injury, when the alarm-gong rang his signal, and tried to go to the fire. The fire-alarms are rung in the hospitals for the information of the ambulance corps. The crippled fireman heard the signal at the dead of night, and, only half awake, jumped out of bed, groped about for the sliding-pole, and, getting hold of the bedpost, tried to slide down that. The plaster cast about his ankle was broken, the old injury reopened, and he was seriously hurt.

New York firemen have a proud saying that they "fight fire from the inside." It means unhesitating courage, prompt sacrifice, and victory gained, all in one. The saving of life that gets into the newspapers and wins applause is done, of necessity, largely from the outside, but is none the less perilous for that. Sometimes, though rarely, it has in its intense gravity almost a comic tinge, as at one of the infrequent fires in the Mulberry Bend some years ago. The Italians believe, with reason, that there is bad luck in fire, therefore do not insure, and have few fires. Of this one the Romolo family shrine was the cause. The lamp upon it exploded, and the tenement was ablaze when the firemen came. The policeman on the beat had tried to save Mrs. Romolo; but she clung to the bedpost, and refused to go without the rest of the family. So he seized the baby, and rolled down the burning stairs with it, his beard and coat afire. The only way out was shut off when the engines arrived. The Romolos shrieked at the top-floor window, threatening to throw themselves out. There was not a moment to be lost. Lying flat on the roof, with their heads over the cornice, the firemen fished the two children out of the window with their hooks. The ladders were run up in time for the father and mother.

The readiness of resource no less than the intrepid courage and athletic skill of the rescuers evoke enthusiastic admiration. Two instances stand out in my recollection among many. Of one Fireman Howe, who had on more than one occasion signally distinguished himself, was the hero. It happened on the morning of January 2, 1896, when the Geneva Club on Lexington Avenue was burned out. Fireman Howe drove Hook-and-Ladder No. 7 to the fire that morning, to find two boarders at the third-story window, hemmed in by flames which already showed behind them. Followed by Fireman Pearl, he ran up in the adjoining building, and presently appeared at a window on the third floor, separated from the one occupied by the two men by a blank wall-space of perhaps four or five feet. It offered no other footing than a rusty hook, but it was enough. Astride of the window-sill, with one foot upon the hook, the other anchored inside by his comrade, his body stretched at full length along the wall, Howe was able to reach the two, and to swing them, one after the other, through his own window to safety. As the second went through, the crew in the street below set up a cheer that raised the sleeping echoes of the street. Howe looked down, nodded, and took a firmer grip; and that instant came his great peril.

A third face had appeared at the window just as the fire swept through. Howe shut his eyes to shield them, and braced himself on the hook for a last effort. It broke; and the man, frightened out of his wits, threw himself headlong from the window upon Howe's neck.

The fireman's form bent and swayed. His comrade within felt the strain, and dug his heels into the boards. He was almost dragged out of the window, but held on with a supreme effort. Just as he thought the end had come, he felt the strain ease up. The ladder had reached Howe in the very nick of time, and given him support. But in his desperate effort to save himself and the other, he slammed his burden back over his shoulder with such force that he went crashing through, carrying sash and all, and fell, cut and bruised, but safe, upon Fireman Pearl, who groveled upon the floor, prostrate and panting.

The other case New York remembers yet
17

with a shudder. It was known long in the department for the bravest act ever done by a fireman—an act that earned for Foreman William Quirk the medal for 1888. He was next in command of Engine No. 22 when, on a March morning, the Elberon Flats in East Eighty-fifth street were burned. The Westlake family, mother, daughter, and two sons, were in the fifth story, helpless and hopeless. Quirk ran up on the scaling-ladder to the fourth floor, hung it on the sill above, and got the boys and their sister down. But the flames burst from the floor below, cutting off their retreat. Quirk's captain had seen the danger, and shouted to him to turn back while it was yet time. But Quirk had no intention of turning back. He measured the distance and the risk with a look, saw the crowd tugging frantically at the life-net under the window, and bade them jump, one by one. They jumped, and were saved. Last of all, he jumped himself, after a vain effort to save the mother. She was already dead. He caught her gown, but the body slipped from his grasp and fell crashing to the street fifty feet below. He himself was hurt in his jump. The volunteers who held the net looked up, and were frightened; they let go their grip,

and the plucky fireman broke a leg and hurt
his back in the fall.

" Like a cry of fire in the night" appeals to
the dullest imagination with a sense of sudden fear.   There have been nights in this city
when the cry swelled into such a clamor of
terror and despair as to make the stoutest
heart quake—when it seemed to those who
had to do with putting out fires as if the end
of all things was at hand.   Such a night was
that of the burning of " Cohnfeld's Folly," in
Bleecker street, March 17, 1891.   The burning
of the big store involved the destruction,
wholly or in part, of ten surrounding buildings, and called out nearly one third of the
city's Fire Department.   While the fire raged
as yet unchecked,—while walls were falling
with shock and crash of thunder, the streets
full of galloping engines and ambulances
carrying injured firemen, with clangor of
urgent gongs; while insurance patrolmen
were being smothered in buildings a block
away by the smoke that hung like a pall over
the city,—another disastrous fire broke out in
the dry-goods district, and three alarm-calls
came from West Seventeenth street.   Nine
other fires were signaled, and before morning
all the crews that were left were summoned

to Allen street, where four persons were
burned to death in a tenement. Those are
the wild nights that try firemen's souls, and
never yet found them wanting. During the
great blizzard, when the streets were impas-
sable and the system crippled, the fires in the
city averaged nine a day,—forty-five for the
five days from March 12 to 16,—and not one
of them got beyond control. The fire commissioners put on record their pride in the
achievement, as well they might. It was
something to be proud of, indeed.

Such a night promised to be the one when
the Manhattan Bank and the State Bank
across the street on the other Broadway
corner, with three or four other buildings,
were burned, and when the ominous "two
nines" were rung, calling nine tenths of the
whole force below Central Park to the threatened quarter. But, happily, the promise was
not fully kept. The supposed fire-proof bank
was crumbling in the withering blast like
so much paper; the cry went up that whole
companies of firemen were perishing within
it; and the alarm had reached Police Headquarters in the next block, where they were
counting the election returns. Thirteen firemen, including the deputy department chief,

a battalion chief, and two captains, limped or
were carried from the burning bank, more or
less injured.   The stone steps of the fire-proof
stairs had fallen with them or upon them.
Their imperiled comrades, whose escape was
cut off, slid down hose and scaling-ladders.
The last, the crew of Engine Company No. 3,
had reached the street, and all were thought
to be out, when the assistant foreman, Daniel
Fitzmaurice, appeared at a fifth-story window.
The fire beating against it drove him away,
but he found footing at another, next adjoining the building on the north.   To reach him
from below, with the whole building ablaze,
was impossible.   Other escape there was none,
save a cornice ledge extending half-way to
his window; but it was too narrow to afford
foothold.

Then an extraordinary scene was enacted
in the sight of thousands.   In the other building were a number of fire-insurance patrolmen, covering goods to protect them against
water damage.   One of these—Patrolman
John Rush—stepped out on the ledge, and
edged his way toward a spur of stone that
projected from the bank building.   Behind
followed Patrolman Barnett, steadying him
and pressing him close against the wall.   Be-

hind him was another, with still another holding on within the room, where the living chain was anchored by all the rest. Rush, at the end of the ledge, leaned over and gave Fitzmaurice his hand. The fireman grasped it, and edged out upon the spur. Barnett, holding the rescuer fast, gave him what he needed—something to cling to. Once he was on the ledge, the chain wound itself up as it had unwound itself. Slowly, inch by inch, it crept back, each man pushing the next flat against the wall with might and main, while the multitudes in the street held their breath, and the very engines stopped panting, until all were safe.

John Rush is a fireman to-day, a member of "Thirty-three's" crew in Great Jones street. He was an insurance patrolman then. The organization is unofficial. Its main purpose is to save property; but in the face of the emergency firemen and patrolmen become one body, obeying one head.

That the spirit which has made New York's Fire Department great equally animates its commercial brother has been shown more than once, but never better than at the memorable fire in the Hotel Royal, which cost so many lives. No account of heroic life-saving at fires, even as fragmentary as this, could pass by the marvelous feat, or feats, of Sergeant (now Captain) John R. Vaughan on that February morning six years ago. The alarm rang in patrol station No. 3 at 3 : 20 o'clock on Sunday morning. Sergeant Vaughan, hastening to the fire with his men, found the whole five-story hotel ablaze from roof to cellar. The fire had shot up the elevator shaft, round which the stairs ran, and from the first had made escape impossible. Men and women were jumping and hanging from windows. One, falling from a great height, came within an inch of killing the sergeant as he tried to enter the building. Darting up into the next house, and leaning out of the window with his whole body, while one of the crew hung on to one leg,—as Fireman Pearl did to Howe's in the splendid rescue at the Geneva Club,—he took a half-hitch with the other in some electric-light wires that ran up the wall, trusting to his rubber boots to protect him from the current, and made of his body a living bridge for the safe passage from the last window of the burning hotel of three men and a woman whom death stared in the face, steadying them as they went with his free hand. As the last passed over,

ladders were being thrown up against the
wall, and what could be done there was
done.

Sergeant Vaughan went up on the roof.
The smoke was so dense there that he could
see little, but through it he heard a cry for
help, and made out the shape of a man standing upon a window-sill in the fifth story,
overlooking the courtyard of the hotel. The
yard was between them. Bidding his men
follow,—they were five, all told,—he ran
down and around in the next street to the
roof of the house that formed an angle with
the hotel wing. There stood the man below
him, only a jump away, but a jump which no
mortal might take and live. His face and
hands were black with smoke. Vaughan,
looking down, thought him a negro. He was
perfectly calm.

"It is no use," he said, glancing up. "Don't
try. You can't do it."

The sergeant looked wistfully about him.
Not a stick or a piece of rope was in sight.
Every shred was used below. There was
absolutely nothing. "But I could n't let
him," he said to me, months after, when he
had come out of the hospital a whole man
again, and was back at work,—"I just

could n't, standing there so quiet and brave."
To the man he said sharply :

"I want you to do exactly as I tell you, now.
Don't grab me, but let me get the first grab."
He had noticed that the man wore a heavy
overcoat, and had already laid his plan.

"Don't try," urged the man.   "You cannot
save me.   I will stay here till it gets too hot;
then I will jump."

"No, you won't," from the sergeant, as he
lay at full length on the roof, looking over.
"It is a pretty hard yard down there.   I will
get you, or go dead myself."

The four sat on the sergeant's legs as he
swung free down to the waist; so he was almost able to reach the man on the window
with outstretched hands.

"Now jump—quick !" he commanded; and
the man jumped.   He caught him by both
wrists as directed, and the sergeant got a grip
on the collar of his coat.

"Hoist !" he shouted to the four on the
roof; and they tugged with their might.   The
sergeant's body did not move.   Bending over
till the back creaked, it hung over the edge, a
weight of two hundred and three pounds suspended from and holding it down.   The cold
sweat started upon his men's foreheads as

they tried and tried again, without gaining an inch. Blood dripped from Sergeant Vaughan's nostrils and ears. Sixty feet below was the paved courtyard; over against him the window, behind which he saw the back-draft coming, gathering headway with lurid, swirling smoke. Now it burst through, burning the hair and the coats of the two. For an instant he thought all hope was gone.

But in a flash it came back to him. To relieve the terrible dead-weight that wrenched and tore at his muscles, he was swinging the man to and fro like a pendulum, head touching head. He could *swing him up!* A smothered shout warned his men. They crept nearer the edge without letting go their grip on him, and watched with staring eyes the human pendulum swing wider and wider, farther and farther, until now, with a mighty effort, it swung within their reach. They caught the skirt of the coat, held on, pulled in, and in a moment lifted him over the edge.

They lay upon the roof, all six, breathless, sightless, their faces turned to the winter sky. The tumult of the street came up as a faint echo; the spray of a score of engines pumping below fell upon them, froze, and covered

them with ice. The very roar of the fire seemed
far off. The sergeant was the first to recover.
He carried down the man he had saved, and
saw him sent off to the hospital. Then first
he noticed that he was not a negro; the smut
had been rubbed off his face. Monday had
dawned before he came to, and days passed
before he knew his rescuer. Sergeant Vaughan
was laid up himself then. He had returned
to his work, and finished it; but what he had
gone through was too much for human
strength. It was spring before he returned
to his quarters, to find himself promoted,
petted, and made much of.

From the sublime to the ridiculous is but a
little step. Among the many who journeyed
to the insurance patrol station to see the hero
of the great fire, there came, one day, a
woman. She was young and pretty, the
sweetheart of the man on the window-sill.
He was a lawyer, since a State senator of
Pennsylvania. She wished the sergeant to
repeat exactly the words he spoke to him in
that awful moment when he bade him jump
—to life or death. She had heard them, and
she wanted the sergeant to repeat them to her,
that she might know for sure he was the man
who did it. He stammered and hitched—tried

subterfuges. She waited, inexorable. Finally, in desperation, blushing fiery red, he blurted out "a lot of cuss-words." "You know," he said apologetically, in telling of it, "when I am in a place like that I can't help it."

When she heard the words which her fiancé had already told her, straightway she fell upon the fireman's neck. The sergeant stood dumfounded. "Women are queer," he said.

Thus a fireman's life. That the very horses that are their friends in quarters, their comrades at the fire, sharing with them what comes of good and evil, catch the spirit of it, is not strange. It would be strange if the did not. With human intelligence and mor than human affection, the splendid anima follow the fortunes of their masters, doin their share in whatever is demanded of them. In the final showing that in thirty years, while with the growing population the number of fires has steadily increased, the average loss per fire has as steadily decreased, they have their full share, also, of the credit. In 1866 there were 796 fires in New Yorl, with an average loss of $8075.38 per fire. In 1876, with 1382 fires, the loss was but $2786.70 at each. In 1896, 3890 fires averaged only $878.81. It means that every year more fires

are headed off than run down—smothered at
the start, as a fire should be. When to the
verdict of "faithful unto death" that record
is added, nothing remains to be said. The
firemen know how much of that is the doing
of their four-legged comrades. It is the one
blot on the fair picture that the city which
owes these horses so much has not seen fit, in
gr titude, to provide comfort for their worn
old age. When a fireman grows old, he is
retired on half-pay for the rest of his days.
When a horse that has run with the heavy
engines to fires by night and by day for perhaps ten or fifteen years is worn out, it is—
old, to a huckster, perhaps, or a contractor,
slave for him until it is fit only for the
ne-yard! The city receives a paltry two or
three thousand dollars a year for this rank
treachery, and pockets the blood-money without a protest. There is room next, in New
Yorl for a movement that shall secure to the
fireman's faithful friend the grateful reward
of a quiet farm, a full crib, and a green pasture to the end of its days, when it is no
longer young enough and strong enough to
"run with the machine."